Anonymous

Voluntaries for an East London Hospital

Anonymous

Voluntaries for an East London Hospital

ISBN/EAN: 9783337230425

Printed in Europe, USA, Canada, Australia, Japan

Cover: Foto ©Andreas Hilbeck / pixelio.de

More available books at **www.hansebooks.com**

VOLUNTARIES

FOR AN EAST LONDON HOSPITAL

BY

THE EARL OF LYTTON, BISHOP OF BEDFORD, E. M. ABDY-WILLIAMS
T. ASHE, C. CHESTON, MRS. W. K. CLIFFORD, AUSTIN DOBSON
ARTHUR GAYE, A. EGMONT HAKE, T. GORDON HAKE
MRS. HECKFORD, W. E. HENLEY, MAY KENDALL
ANDREW LANG, WALTER POLLOCK
F. MABEL ROBINSON, EDWARD ROSE
CLEMENT SCOTT, R. L. STEVENSON
J. L. TOOLE.

LONDON
DAVID STOTT, 370, OXFORD STREET, W
1887

INTRODUCTORY NOTE.

THIS volume is given to the public by its promoter, Mrs. Charles Cheston, in the hope that the East London Hospital for Children, in aid of which it has been produced, will materially benefit by the proceeds of its sale.

Mrs. Cheston asked me to assist her in the quest of good material to lay before the reader, and wishes me now to offer her warmest thanks to the many distinguished writers who have contributed to this book. At the same time she gives me this opportunity to record my own grateful recognition of the kindness of those who, in answer to my appeals, have so promptly and graciously given of their treasures for the sake of East London's suffering poor.

H. B. DONKIN.

June, 1887.

B *

East London Hospital for Children,

SHADWELL.

——:o:——

PATRONS.

HER MOST GRACIOUS MAJESTY THE QUEEN.

GENERAL COMMITTEE.

BOARD OF MANAGEMENT.

SECRETARY.

CONTENTS.

THE STORY OF THE EAST LONDON
HOSPITAL FOR CHILDREN.

BY MRS. HECKFORD.

I HAVE been asked to write a short account of the
East London Hospital for Children, and having
consented, I must, before beginning, ask the in-
dulgence of all who read it.

In the entrance hall of the hospital is a large
tablet with this inscription :

In Memory of
Nathaniel Heckford, M.D., M.R.C.S.
Born in Calcutta, April, 1842
Died 14th December, 1871
Aged 29
He Founded this Institution
At His Own Cost
In a Warehouse at Ratcliff Cross
January 28, 1868
He Lived For It
And Died
A Few Days After The Site
Of This Building was
Purchased by the
Committee of Management of the
Hospital.

It is not a mortuary tablet, but a beautiful mosaic of Venetian manufacture, and the golden ground, rich colouring, and Egyptian alabaster bring a vision of San Marco and of Venice, when she was the bond between stern European facts and gorgeous Eastern idealism, before the eyes of those gifted with a little learning and some imagination. For the rest of those who look at it, it is but a fantastically graceful memorial contrasting strangely with its surroundings, and telling of the Eastern birth, short life, and single-minded devotion to the hospital of a man, the memory of whose unusual beauty of disposition and form still appeals to the untutored imaginations of numbers of poor toilers in the grime of Ratcliff and Shadwell.

I cannot tell the story of the hospital's life without telling his, nor his without in part telling my own and those of others, for an institution lives in the human hope, love, and aspiration that strive to express themselves through it, and its biography is to be found in the lives of those whose happiness and woe have ebbed and flowed from and around it ; to whom it has been as a living creature, to be tended lovingly, to be looked to in time of need as a trusty friend ; a thing to be cherished and relied upon, to be wept over and prayed for ; a thing worth living and dying for.

In the year 1866 Nathaniel Heckford was a surgeon and doctor at the London Hospital. He had carried off all the honours possible during his student days, taking the gold medal for surgery and medicine in the same year. His devotion to his profession, his chivalrous championship of the weak or oppressed, and his unselfishness to all, rendered him a favourite alike with his teachers, his patients, and his comrades. When the cholera broke out in the summer of that year he volunteered to help a friend, Dr. Woodman, who was in charge of the Wapping District Cholera Hospital ; and there I first met him, I being also a volunteer, in the capacity of nurse : in addition to which I was a student of medicine.

We soon became friends, for in his spare moments he was always ready to talk of his patients' cases, of their individual joys and woes, or to drift into speculations, moral, social, or religious, showing an absence of conventionality in his ideas, and a fearlessness in following his thought, to whatever end it tended, which was almost startling; whilst perhaps a moment after he would exhibit an appreciation of fun and a childlike pleasure in trifles which contrasted strangely with his more serious moods. He was a great favourite in the hospital with both patients and nurses, and from the latter I heard of his devotion to the out-door sufferers—of how he never thought it trouble to go out at any hour if he could be of use; and, further, a little trait of his consideration for creatures not human, namely, for that domestic plague, a black-beetle, the life of one of which I was told half indignantly, he had rescued, saying that death was probably as disagreeable to the beetle as it would be to him. I heard also that he described himself as an " Indian," and I remarked that his ideas and even his modes of expression were tinged with Orientalism.

From the maze of figures which rise before me as I recall this time, one stands out prominently. Margarite (I spell her name as she spelt it) was the servant in the doctor's room, and used to bring me my dinner from thence. I can see her now as she first

attracted my notice—a delicately-formed girl of seven-
teen, with a small refined face and dark hair and
eyes. She was leaning on the stair balustrade outside the ward—a ray of sunlight heavily laden with
motes gilding her hair, whilst it threw her face into
soft shadow; her arms were bared to the elbow, and
her taper fingers peeped from under the white apron
carelessly thrown over them, as she stood there
droopingly, her dark lashes resting on her pale
cheeks—and quite unconscious that she was making
a charming picture.

One evening shortly before the cholera wore itself
out, Mr. Heckford, as he was walking to my lodgings
with me, said he had a favour to ask, if I would grant
it. He told me that he was much interested in
Margarite, that he thought her a very superior girl,
and that he knew she was doomed by consumption if
she were not removed from her actual surroundings.
He asked me if I could help her in any way, for that
he could not : saying frankly, that he had no money,
and that his recommendation would do her no good
with anyone he knew but me. We then planned that
she should be sent to my sister's and my house in the

West End, there to be trained under our lady's-maid.

Thus Margarite became a legacy of the Cholera Hospital. On the 28th January, 1867, I was married to Mr. Heckford, and we took the girl for our servant.

We determined to work out our theories of life as it ought to be, on thoroughly new principles; we were somewhat undetermined as to what to do, but we agreed that we must do something to show how much happiness might ensue if persons of means and culture would devote themselves to elevating those less fortunate than they.

Almost everyone expected that my husband would enter the career of a consulting surgeon in the West End; but the life of a fashionable medical man offered no attractions to him. It was not the first time that he had turned carelessly from what would have allured most men.

" What is the greatest result you look forward to in that sort of life ? " he said to me; " why do you want me to go in for it ? The most it would lead to would be our wasting our time trying to please people, instead of trying to help them ; in our frittering away in ostentatious living almost as much money as we should make, and in giving parties to people we should not care for, and who would not care for us ; and then at the end perhaps I should become Sir Nathaniel Heckford. What a glorious ambition! Let us stop and work in the East End—it will be much better."

It was the same with his sending notes of his cases to the medical papers, or contemplating writing a book on any special subject. He was often urged to bring his name forward by men who knew how much success depends on a name being often before the public. " When I have any really instructive case," he would say, " I will bring it forward. What good will it do to bring my name forward ? That is what fills up more than half the medical papers—men puffing themselves."

One evening, when the days were already short, he came home rather late from a visit he had been paying at the London Hospital to some men on the resident staff. " I tell you what we must do," he said, " we must start a Children's Hospital.

It is the thing most needed, and will do the most good. It is *the* great need of the East End, and we must do that and nothing else ! "

Then began the search for premises. My husband in his spare time, and Margarite and I at all times, tramped daily over the parishes of Shadwell, Ratcliff, and Stepney, in what seemed a hopeless quest. At last a Dissenting minister of the name of Benn told us of two old warehouses at Ratcliff Cross, close to the river. The price asked was £2,000, an exorbitant sum, but we were so hopeless of finding anything else, and so impatient to begin, that we agreed to it.

It was delightful work now. We moved our furniture, and electrified Ratcliff Cross by the sight of the van and its contents. Some of the articles were too large to pass up the narrow stairs, and had to be hoisted through the windows, whilst a crowd of excited youngsters in the street acted chorus as each article was removed from the van, crying, " Here comes the sofa ! Here come the fenders ! Oh ! look at the gold, oh !—" their minds not having yet grasped the idea " all is not gold that glitters," which delusion also caused our little drawing-room to be described by one privileged to see it as being "all furnished in gold," owing to a buhl cabinet and some ormolu ornaments. When our rooms were settled they looked very pretty; in the ward above them ten little iron bedsteads awaited their inmates; I painted " East London Hospital for Children and Dispensary for Women " on a board; we fixed it above the warehouse door, and on the 28th January, 1868, the first anniversary of our wedding day, the hospital was opened.

It soon increased in every way. We were crowded with " in " and " out " patients, and my husband gave up his private practice, partly in order to devote all his time to the hospital, partly because he wished to avoid suspicion of using it as a means to push him-self professionally before the public. We hardly knew how the time went, and took but little count of it ; indeed, we worked so late, and were called up from our sleep so often, that day and night got some-what mixed up ; added to which, I often went out to attend women in their confinements, and my husband constantly attended patients at their own homes, besides doing amateur work as a nightly visitor in haunts where the police were afraid to go alone. It was dangerous, no doubt, and I always felt thankful when he came home safe: but he had a great influence over the people, and it was a part of our scheme for reforming the neighbourhood. No one who did not live near the Ratcliff Highway then can have an idea of what it was. I have seen men and women fighting and rolling together in the gutter before the hospital doors; have heard the shrieks of a woman in an opposite house until they were stopped by her being felled to the ground, and left weltering in her blood, by her drunken husband, whilst her children stood aside in terror; and although we could see all from the windows of the wards, have been powerless to interfere because the poor creature had not called "Murder!" I have seen my husband stand unarmed in the midst of a yelling mob, which the police were afraid to approach, and have heard his voice rise above the din and quell it, whilst he appealed to the better nature of those wild men and women; until at last they would disperse, the very combatants bidding him "Good-night, and God bless

you, sir!" But as time went on the civilizing effect
of the hospital began to be felt. I do not wish to
paint these poor people as better than they are, but
I think it speaks volumes in favour of the wretched
population seething around " The Highway," that not
only my husband, but that I also, *alone*, have traversed
their streets and alleys at all hours of the night and
early morning, with a watch and gold chain round
my neck, a diamond ring on my finger, and a valuable brooch fastening my dress, yet have never been
molested.

If we saw dreadful scenes, we also saw much
laughter and merriment. We were a band of friends,
with but little distinction of social rank kept up between us, although we enforced strict discipline;
there was not an elderly person in the whole establishment, and where all are young and are heart and
soul in a common work, mirth is sure to be. It was
wonderful how the girls or young women (for we had
no man-servant at first) seemed to grasp the idea of
friendship without familiarity, and how enthusiastically
they embraced the thought of endeavouring to help
others rather than themselves. Perhaps they were

kept too busy to have time to quarrel, but certain
it is we never had bickerings to contend with. Soon
we opened another ward, on the top storey of the
second house. It was a babies' ward, and was a new
feature altogether; for, until we set the example, no
child under two years old was admitted as a hospital
inmate.

The work was soon as much as we could get
through with; but my husband was still impatient
to push on, so we opened the fourth or bottom ward,
and by means of partitions turned the ground floor of
the second house into a nurse's sitting-room, a small
office, and a store-room for the various garments
which began now to be sent to us. We were also
obliged to engage a house opposite for sleeping ac-
commodation, as the increasing staff of nurses and
servants was becoming seriously cramped.

I cannot but linger lovingly over the remembrance
of our nurses and servants, for without their devotion
we should never have made the hospital a success, and
further, because they taught me a lesson which has
been to me of great value.

It is often said in good faith that the distinction of

rank lies below the surface, and that it is not merely a difference of polish. This is a mistake, but a mistake so easy to make, and so difficult to avoid, that, except under very unusual circumstances, it is an inevitable one. As a rule, when a person of education, refinement, and wealth, encourages an intimate acquaintance with a social and educational inferior, one of the two endeavours to accommodate his or her perception to the habitual mental focus of the other. A housemaid who endeavours to look at life from the same point of view as her fashionable mistress, becomes absurd, and *vice versâ.* The natural aspect of things is disturbed through faulty vision, and their efforts at understanding each other tend to separate instead of uniting them; but let circumstances arise which cause the mistress and servant to be united in one great common interest which gives them a common focus, and they will soon understand that the distinctions of social rank depend solely on polish, and that there is as much refinement and elevation of thought to be found in the homes of the poor as of the rich. It is a difficult idea to grasp, unless in the midst of such work as ours was. The

c *

beauty of a thought, inelegantly or inadequately expressed, is often lost to the hearer, and but half appreciated by the speaker; yet its lustre is revealed if it can but express itself in action instead of in words. It is the same with sentiment. How frequently does one hear it said that the poor have not the same amount of feeling as the rich. It seems a true remark often; yet, in action, the poor will show a perseverance in endurance and toil for the sake of a loved one that few rich persons ever contemplate. A rugged face does not, as a rule, lend itself to the delicate changes which betoken emotion, neither is an untaught tongue able to form words to express ideas; nay, more than this, the terrible exigencies of a life of grinding poverty blunt that sense of the fitness of things which gives the finishing touch to a picture of joy or woe. It is not until we stand side by side in our daily work with the hewers of wood and drawers of water that we realize how much our leisure enables us to study dramatic effect in all that goes to make up life. A woman who has to lock her baby's corpse into the only cupboard she has, along with the bread and sugar, in order to prevent her remaining little ones from wasting her scanty stores, or being frightened at the dead body whilst she is away at the hospital waiting for the certificate of death ; a man who cannot but allow his wife's corpse to be opened in his own room, perhaps lying on his one table, in order that the professional scruples of her medical attendant may be satisfied before giving the same necessary document; or a child who hears the most private concerns of its parents' life ruthlessly discussed by a parish officer, is liable to harden on the outside ; but within there may be, and often is, as refined a nature as can be found amongst the most delicately nurtured ladies or gentlemen.

I could fill a large volume with tales revealing this fact, though in this short sketch I can say but this, that we exercised no particular selection in taking girls into the hospital to train, many of them being chosen rather on account of their need of help than because they appeared particularly desirable ; yet that the moral tone of the establishment was so high that servants would confess their own delinquencies, and pay the fine imposed on

C 2 *

them in consequence, when they might have escaped punishment by silence; that a domestic rebellion took place to force us to provide more delicate food for our own use than was allowed in the kitchen, our plan being to fare alike throughout; and that in a place where theft was particularly easy, and where the temptations to it were great, it was practically unknown. " It is not my work," was a remark never heard in the hospital. If a thing had to be done, it was done by whoever had time and ability to do it; and the intelligence displayed by even very young girls in learning to perform such services as in large hospitals are entrusted to " dressers," was remarkable.

Margarite distinguished herself particularly. She studied anatomy in her leisure hours, learned the use of the stethoscope, and attended at the *post mortems*. She was an invaluable nurse ; gentle, merry, but firm, and with a brightness of intelligence that seemed to render new ideas her own in a surprisingly short space of time, she soon came to be our right hand in everything regarding the patients. Our only anxiety respecting her was her health ; this sometimes obliged us to remove her from her work, much against her own will, although she was aware of the extent of her delicacy. I remember her startling us once in the *post mortem* room. We were examining the lungs of a patient who had died of a peculiar form of consumption, when suddenly she said, " That is the same sort of case as mine, sir, I think, only worse ? " The purely scientific interest expressed in her voice and look as she asked the question impressed us both forcibly.

We had not long opened the fourth and last ward before we found that funds were running short. We were spending our entire private income, and even trenching on capital, in order to supplement the hospital funds ; but, about the same time, we made two good friends — Dr. Murray and his cousin, Mr. Anderson. Dr. Murray had been appointed by the editor of the *British Medical Journal* to report on various hospitals, amongst others on the " London." My husband made his acquaintance, and asked him to visit our bantling. He was to come to lunch, and go over the hospital afterwards.

We seldom indulged in luxuries, and our cooking was of the simplest ; but this being a special occasion

we determined to rise to it, and, in solemn conclave
with the cook, I determined to attempt strawberry
tartlets. The excitement produced in the kitchen
by this announcement was great: it was generally
felt that a superior effort was about to be made for
the good of the hospital.

Dr. Murray came and partook, all unconsciously, of
the tartlets. Whilst he was in the wards, after lunch,
Mr. Heckford descended to the subterranean kitchen
to see that all was in order there. It was an unevenly
paved, murky apartment at best—a cellar in disguise,
but at that particular moment an accidental slip of
the foot had upset a pailful of water which made
small pools in the inequalities of the floor. " Wipe it
up, quick," said my husband; " Dr. Murray is just
coming down. You'll get us a bad report." " What !"
exclaimed the girl addressed, " after all them tarts ? "

The report, however, was a good one; and not
only that, but Dr. Murray subsequently helped us in
many other ways.

Shortly after this Mr. Charles Dickens paid a visit
to the hospital, and then the excitement was general.
The cook, who was fat, hid herself, and peeped at

Mr. Dickens from a retired corner, having, as she explained afterwards, a dread of being "took off" by the great novelist. After leaving the hospital he went with my husband to visit some of our poor neighbours, and in a few days he sent me the proof-slips of an article he had written on our hospital and them. It came one evening whilst I was out, and I found it on the table on my return. I opened it with a trembling hand: it is needless to say that it was beautiful. When did that marvellous writer pen anything that was not beautiful, or fail to touch the chords of the heart?

The article appeared on the 19th December, 1868, and the last post of that same day brought a letter to my husband in a round childish hand, in which the writer told her " Dear Mr. Heckford " that her mamma had read the story of his hospital to her, that she was only a little girl of six, but would like to give him the contents of her money-box for the little children, and signed herself his " affectionate little May." I have that letter still. It was the poetical beginning of an influx of money and other help. The next day, and for long after, letters flowed in so rapidly that we had difficulty in answering them quickly enough. The help came just in time, and the relief from excessive anxiety was in itself a shock. We determined to give a grand Christmas party : two hundred of the poor around were invited. A member of our Committee kindly provided a magic lantern, and a few friends came from the West-End. We had a Christmas-tree in the operating theatre, and a grand tea in the out-patients' room, where the magic lantern was subsequently displayed. We made the nurses exquisitely happy by presenting them with white book-muslin dresses and red sashes, in which they looked charming, and we fixed the day for Christmas Eve. Everything was most successful : the hospital, decorated with flags and evergreens, offered a quaint appearance filled with motley guests. Our poorer friends were delighted at seeing the pretty dresses of those who were richer, and also the unusual attire of the nurses. We had a Punch, with a Dog Toby, and a barrel-organ for music. There were but few dangerous cases in the wards at the time, and many of our little patients were brought downstairs to enjoy the fun after the Christmas-tree was dismantled.

I must here pay a tribute to Mr. Julius Cæsar.

He was only a lad, and nominally was our volunteer dispenser, but really he was the life of the hospital. Nothing ever came amiss to him : if I wanted anything done, I was sure to ask Julius, and if a toddling baby in the wards wanted anything done, it very probably asked Julius also. " Mr. Cæsar," was a household word in many a poor home in those days, and even now is not forgotten. The little patients, and the nurses and servants, idolized him. His advent in the ward, whither he always betook himself after dinner, was heralded by a shriek of delight and a universal romp ; and many a time he would catch up a baby and run downstairs with it sitting on his shoulder, to show it the glories of our private apartments, whilst on the occasion of impromptu festivities in honour of the birth-days of our nurses and servants, his genius for making people enjoy themselves was invaluable.

But in spite of all our fun, not only my husband, but Margarite and I were beginning to suffer from over-work and anxiety, Margarite most of all. Just then, an American lady, Mrs. Johnson, a friend of Charles Dickens, asked us to recommend a nice trustworthy girl to be a maid and playfellow to her little daughter, who, with one much older, was to accompany her in a tour through France, Italy, and Switzerland. After some consultation we determined to ask her to take Margarite, on the understanding that the girl was to receive no wages, but was not to be treated as an ordinary servant, and was, if necessary, to have the extra comforts required by an invalid. We arranged to provide her with dress allowance and pocket money, and Mrs. Johnson acceded.

It was evidently the last chance to save Margarite's life, for she was drooping rapidly. We provided her with a little travelling library, and she started on her new life. As letter after letter came home, we read them with ever increasing astonishment. It was difficult to imagine that the writer was the Margarite of but two years back. The girl's writing and spelling had always been good; but not until we read these letters did we realize what a development had taken place. Mrs. Johnson acted in a spirit of true American liberality : Margarite was worthy of being a member of her family, and she treated her as one.

Christmas was coming round again—but Christmas laden with terrible anxieties. Money was not coming in, and our expenses, both as regarded the hospital and our private arrangements, were increased. We retrenched in every way we could, planned and re-planned how we could make a shilling do duty for one-and-sixpence ; but when, close on Christmas, we paid our monthly accounts, all we had in hand was two-and-eleven-pence of the hospital funds, and a balance of two or three pounds at our bankers. It was evident that we could not go on, and it was decided despairingly to close two of the wards and discharge some of our nurses. When the fatal de-cision was known, the whole staff of the hospital came to us as a deputation, even to the last scrubber, whose face, I remember, was streaked with grimy tears. They would serve for nothing—we might cut down whatever could be cut down in their food—they would trust to our paying them what we could when the money began again to come in—anything, not to shut the wards. I forget who were spokes-women, but I know there were many sobs and tears when we explained that it would be an unavailing

sacrifice ; for that it was not the small wages we paid
that constituted the difficulty, but the keep of the
patients.

There was an amateur entertainment given at the
" London " on a certain evening, in aid of the funds
of that institution. Although the fiat for reducing
our little hospital had gone forth, we had yet made
no change. We were invited to the entertainment,
and went, although little disposed for merriment. It
was a brilliant little affair. We walked home
gloomily. The day was close at hand when the wards
must be cleared ; and it seemed so hard to think
that the rich " London " was being fed whilst our
little struggling hospital was dying of starvation. We
had no heart left even for lament, and we
walked in silence. I was taking off my bonnet in my
room when my husband came in quickly, waving a
letter in his hand. " What do you think this is ? " he
asked. " A thousand pounds ! " " Nonsense ; how
can you talk so ? I exclaimed ; but he held it before
my eyes : it was—it really was a note for one
thousand pounds — sent anonymously ! The relief
was so great that our entire household was stunned

by it ; nor do I remember any rejoicing until the next day.

As Christmas came on great preparations were made for our treat. The tree promised to be magnificent with the toys sent by kind friends. We had nightly rehearsals of the carols to be sung by children in costume ; a special Punch and Judy was to be provided by one of our Committee ; a brass band from one of the schools was to perform ; there was to be a tea for the children in the out-patients' room, and supper for the grown-up people in the kitchen, which was to be illuminated with Chinese lamps. Numbers of friends of the hospital came to this party, amongst others an artist from the *Illustrated News.* It was a great success, but it struck me, even at the time, that there was a new and faulty element in it. There was no longer that perfect feeling of accord in one, and only one, object between those who in one way or another represented the hospital,—the object, namely, of giving as much pleasure as possible to the poorer guests. There were some who were thinking simply of amusing themselves, and others of what effect was being produced by the scene on persons who might support the charity. I could hardly have put the idea into words then, but ·I felt it. We were beginning to be touched with the disease that kills so many institutions. Nevertheless, the success was grand as far as the poor were concerned ; and years after I heard a woman who was there recount how she and her husband had that night seen what they had never seen before or since—ladies in evening dress ; and how they had been regaled on turkey and champagne in a room lit by Chinese lamps. I did not destroy the harmless illusion, but my memory must be strangely at .fault if there were either turkey or champagne provided, although I know there was some very weak mulled wine ; the glamour of the unusual sight around her acted like a fairy's wand, I imagine, in respect of the viands.

The new year brought with it the certainty that Mr. Heckford was in consumption, and the more he felt his strength failing the more feverishly impatient did he become to see the hospital's life ensured. Like all impatience it defeated its object, for it sapped his strength and power of work, whilst subscriptions were falling off, and the committee seemed lacking in initiative.

"There is but one thing," he said to me one evening when he was greatly dispirited ; "they wont pull together until they know that the place absolutely belongs to them; they have some idea that we want to put *our*selves forward. Let us give them the freehold ; they *must* work then." I demurred, and suggested giving a nominal leasehold ; but he did not think that would suffice. The matter dropped ; but as the clouds gathered fast, he reverted again and again to it. "We shall neither of us live long," he would say in answer to my reminding him that by giving the freehold he deprived himself for ever of the right to dispose of the premises, which we had already determined that it was imperative to leave as soon as we could collect enough money to purchase ground for and erect a new building. It had been his original intention that when the Children's Hospital was "started" in a more suitable home the old warehouses should be utilised as a Lock Hospital for Women, in the hope of thereby being able to combat evil morally as well as physically ;

but now he resigned the idea as hopeless. " We shall never live to do it," he said. " Let us make sure of the future of our one scheme ; we shall never do more, if even we can manage that : if we die before it is fairly started it will be ruined. The Committee *must* work, and they won't till they feel the place is theirs." I knew there was a great deal of truth in what he said ; but the conviction that was growing on me that his life was being worn out by his desperate anxiety regarding the hospital at last wrung consent from me.

The deed was drawn up and signed, but the good resulting from the excitement and astonishment caused by our unexpected gift was ephemeral.

It was just then, at our utmost need, that the gentleman who has ever since been our Secretary was appointed, and I soon knew that a more experienced hand than either of ours was on the helm of the hospital bark.

The life of fun and frolic was gradually fading away like the dew of early morning before the noon-day glare. We could not understand why this should be, and we rebelled fiercely against it : it was in some

ways a nineteenth-century version of Jonah and the
gourd in the days of Nineveh. "The hospital"
meant to us—not a mere hospital, however well
appointed and well managed,—it meant a system by
which widely different classes of society might come
to appreciate their unity, and learn to develop the
good which is in all alike, disguised under varied
aspects. I doubt whether my husband could have
formulated the idea in words,—I know I could not at
that time ; but "the hospital" formulated it in action,
and was its true practical expression. No Committee
can be blamed for finding it impossible to realize this
idea, yet in this fact lies, I think, the great danger of
all charitable institutions, a danger that can be averted
by individual effort, but which must be recognized in
order to be averted, and which it would be well if
every subscriber to such an institution should think
upon. Guineas alone do not give life to institutions,
any more than to their inmates; the gold must be
given, doubtless, but so must the sympathy, which
can come but by personal contact. As day after day
we met the Secretary in the office, and marked how
calmly, firmly, and conscientiously he did his work—

D *

never being in a hurry, but always being ready,—we wondered whether he would be able to take up our idea, and help us to work it out.

By the end of the autumn my husband's health was so shattered that he was ordered to winter either in Italy or Egypt. We only got as far as beautiful Amalfi, and settled down in the quaint and comfortable hotel of the Capucini, where he revived. We were lulled in a smiling haven, but outside the storm was rising, and I felt sure my husband would soon put out into it again. Our letters from England were not at all reassuring, and our anxiety became daily greater and greater. My husband watched feverishly for letters,—even telegrams once passed between Amalfi and London ; and when finally, in February, we received some important and startling news, he determined to return home.

How well I remember when he finally arrived at this decision ! It was a beautiful evening, and I had been sitting on the balcony for a long while, gazing at the enchanting view, which was becoming more and more fairy-like as the sun lowered, and as each headland and bay, each pinnacled rock or tangled break of that fretted coast caught a transient gleam of sunlight, or was thrown into purple shade. My thoughts had been sad enough, but I was entranced by the magic of the scene. My husband joined me, and stood leaning on the balcony: suddenly he turned—" Well," he said, " when shall we start?" It was like the tolling of a death-bell, breaking the spell which bound me. With all that soft loveliness tempting him to stay, it seemed cruel that he must go back in the teeth of the March winds.

I took the situation all to pieces, and ended by saying that I *would* not, *could* not advise, but that he must see that it was useless for him to go back unless he meant to put himself into hard work at once, which, in his state of health, meant certain death within the year. He might right the hospital by a supreme effort, and die ; or he might wait, leave it to its fate, whatever that might be ; regain his strength, and be able to work for years. " But the hospital would be ruined," he said. I could make no reply. My faith in a Providence of which we are at best but instruments, and often mere

D 2 *

tools, was very faint and vague.   I believed in him,
and in myself, practically more than I believed in anything else.   He stood for a while, gazing dreamily
over the blue sea, then turned from it.   "We will
go home," he said, at last ; "what you say is true,
I shall not see next year, but the hospital will
be saved !   What is my life against the good of
numbers?   'The hospital must go first.'"   By the
time we reached England he was once more ill.   I
have no doubt we made more of the difficulties and
dangers surrounding the hospital's career than was
reasonable, yet, looking back, I still adhere to my
husband's opinion   that he was right in returning
home.

Shortly after, Margarite returned to England, and
paid us a flying visit as she passed through London
on her way to Torquay with Mrs. Johnson.   We were
a short way out of town at the time, and I drove to
the station to meet her.   The train arrived and a young
lady came quickly forward.   I almost gasped.   It was
our Margarite, yet not our Margarite.   Even before
she spoke there was that indescribable something
about her which is so seldom met with but in

one who, if not born, has been, at least, from childhood, bred a "lady." But Margarite was one; by every turn of her face and figure, by every action, every word, even by the intonation of her voice. It was a triumph; and my husband and I rejoiced over it accordingly. But our rejoicing was very spasmodical now. Anxieties of all sorts pressed heavily on us.

Before the autumn was ended, Mr. Heckford achieved what he had longed for : the site which he had months before chosen as being the most suitable for the new hospital, was agreed to by the Committee, and purchased. Plans for the new building were ordered to be drawn out, and a fresh and complete set of rules, suitable for permanently working an institution by, was under consideration. Then he broke down completely. At the last Committee meeting in October, unable any longer to leave him, even for a few hours, I asked for leave of absence from my post of Visiting Governor, and went with him to Ramsgate. There he seemed to revive for a few days. Julius came down to cheer us, and made the place bright, as he always did, by his light-hearted

unselfishness.   The Secretary came also for two days.
I remember, during this visit, his making a remark
which struck me so forcibly that it has since influenced
me much.   I said that I " believed " something, and
he objected to my use of the word.   " If you consider," he said, " you do not believe it.   We say that
we believe many things ; but our actions prove often
that not only do we not believe them, but that we
believe the reverse.   Nothing is believed in which is
not made the basis for action."   I, of course, cannot
repeat the words exactly, but the sense I have
rendered.   It struck me as a great and novel truth—
one worth thinking of; I wondered I had never
thought of it before, and I repeat it here, deeming that
others too may never have thought of it.

At last my husband was confined to his bed.   Even
there he worked at amendments to the rules, which
had been sent to us in slip.   An important meeting
of Committee was expected to take place on the 12th
of December.   He insisted that I must leave him to
be present at it ; and I went.   It was night before I
reached Ramsgate.   My husband's first words were a
question as to the result of the Committee.   He had

been lying with the watch beside him during the day, impatient for the time when he knew that I should be speaking. He knew he was dying, and was at times delirious; indeed he had known for some time that there was no more hope. " I have done so little," he said once, "and I hoped to do so much; but I suppose it was worth living for to do but that little?" Shortly before he died, he told me that I must try to feel that it was better for him to die than to live, for that, broken as his health was, he should only cause me to waste money and thought in carrying a worn-out creature from place to place, instead of devoting both to helping those who might yet be useful. "You will be able to do much more good without me than with me," he ended. " You will not be long in following me, but you must see the hospital settled." He breathed his last on the morning of the 14th December. Before his body was laid in our family grave at Woking, it lay for a day in his old consulting-room in the hospital, where crowds of women and children came to weep over it.

A year after Margarite passed away. Unable to

bear the inaction of the life she was leading in the
house of a dear friend of mine, where she had remained
after Mrs. Johnson left for America, whither Margarite
could not accompany her on account of the cold, she
besought me to let her go once more to the hospital.
"You will not be alive in three months time if you
do," I said. She threw herself on her knees by my
side. "Do not think me ungrateful," she said, kissing my hands; "but I claim it as a right to be
useful. My idleness is against all Mr. Heckford taught
me to know as right—all that you yourself hold as
right. Let me go! I am not afraid of death." She
was greeted with delight by the doctors, who
knew her worth, and worked until she fell in the
ward, from weakness, as she was going to tend a
patient. Her body lies in a grave beside that of my
husband in the Woking Cemetery.

In the summer of 1875 the foundation stone of the
new hospital was laid; in the autumn of the following
year the new building was finished and the tablet
placed in the hall. It was the signal for my final
abdication of all guardianship over our child. The
building was not yet inhabited when I bade farewell

to the life I have told of, and to Europe. Before I
left, the Secretary and I went over the empty building
together. We lingered lovingly over each little
detail, even to the gnarled markings on the massive
and polished wooden doors. It seemed so strange to
stand in that beautiful new place, and to think of the
once struggling life of the little old hospital; strange,
too, to think that a new sort of life—a life utterly
ignorant or forgetful of all that had made this place
what it was, would soon be pouring through the
passages where now our footsteps echoed. As we
stood there together, I felt that, for the nonce, this
eldest daughter of my hopes and fears belonged
equally to us ; but that she was decked for her bridal,
and that even as a mother parts with her daughter to
the man who has nobly won her heart, with something of pain but more of thankfulness, so I was
about to surrender the future hospital to this friend
of mine, for he had won the right to call it his
by the self-denying devotion and the untiring work of
brain and hand of which this building was the result.
There was a pang in the thought that the time would
come when our very names would be forgotten by

those who would dwell within these walls, and pass to and fro through these passages; but it was momentary, for I knew that as long as that building stood, so long would the tablet in the hall tell of the one to whom that hospital would be a monument, of one without whose vivifying touch we two should never have awakened to the happiness that is to be found in living for an idea, even if the effort to express it in action be fraught with sorrow and disappointment.

Nearly eleven years have passed since that day, and I have passed far away from all that hospital circle; but a child never loses its right to call for its mother's help; the hospital has called for mine, and trifling though it be, I give what I can from my heart.

It is to mothers and fathers that I appeal. Our hospital still takes into its wards babies under two years old, whom no other hospital will admit because they are so troublesome and so expensive; still admits little children doomed before their admission to swell its death-rate and its expenditure, preferring the true glory of alleviating moral and physical suffering to the false glory of flattering statistics.

Think of this when standing by the cot of your

healthy darling, or whilst trying to lull the fretful cry
of your ailing one; when its little life is hanging in the
balance, and nothing on earth but the lavish expenditure of money can save it for you, or ease its last
moments with you. Statistics are dry, but glance at
those appended, and think if the sickliest baby ever
seen in a rich nursery could compare with the misery
of the little creatures, bred and cradled in abject
want, who come to the hospital pleading for some
respite to their sufferings. They will be the fellow-
citizens of your children in days to come; will you
not try to help them to some gentle memories that
may soothe the bitterness of the life that is before
them? For these little things often come to the hospital
again and again when the pressure of misery breeds
disease in their frail bodies, are tided over their
infancy and childhood, and come to be men and
women, such as those who sometimes stop me in the
street and ask hesitatingly if I am not the wife of the
doctor at the old Children's Hospital, and if I do not
remember "little Johnny," or "the little girl as
you used to call 'Dolly.'" Think, too, of what a
treasure it would be to one, who, like our Resident

Medical Officer, is fighting, and for the last six years has fought, for the lives of these children, if he had the means of giving something more than medicine to cases which cannot be admitted, or which are discharged cured, but which are being, or going to be, starved, through no fault of their own or of their parents. Think what an awful weight of sorrow rests on a man who feels with, but cannot relieve, the sufferings caused to his patients by hunger. I am pleading not only for subscriptions to an Hospital Extension Fund, but for a Samaritan Fund to be placed at the disposal of the Resident Medical Officer. Men in that position cannot be imposed upon by mock distress, and those who, like Mr. Scott Battams, work, year in year out, amongst scenes of woe without becoming callous, are gradually killed by the overstrain; it is worth thinking of even from a utilitarian point of view, for surely men who unostentatiously form a link of sympathy between riches and poverty are bulwarks of public safety. And let me beg of all those who buy this book to read and ponder the following letter addressed last year by Mr. Battams to the Committee of the hospital : there is no sentimental trapping around the facts mentioned ; their awful pathos, written in this rich and Christian land, wants none.

GENTLEMEN,

I have the honour to lay before you for the fifth time my yearly classified Report of In-Patients of this hospital. Of 950 children admitted into the hospital, 346 were *infants* of two years and under ; no less than 195 being of one year and under. There were nearly 100 babies under six months. There have been 209 deaths ; 144 occurring in infants under two years of age. Of these children, 33 died before the second day ; and 23 died a few hours after admission. During the past year the work of the hospital has been rendered more difficult and more anxious by reason of the terrible increase in the poverty and destitution in this—the poorest—district of London. Diseases have been rendered more severe and more hopeless. Half-starved and half-clothed children have been admitted in large numbers ; and not the least distressing feature of our work has been the returning of these children to their squalid homes after having surrounded them with every comfort. A larger number of parents have been forced to apply to the parish authorities to bury their children than in any previous year. Those who know most of the poor will best understand the full significance of the fact.

I am, Gentlemen,

Your obedient Servant

J. SCOTT BATTAMS,

Resident Medical Officer.

To the Board of Management,
East London Hospital for Children.

WEIGHTS OF TWO HUNDRED AND FIFTY CHILDREN.

Taken consecutively and without selection from the Hospital Books.

AGE.	NUMBER WEIGHED.	LOWEST WEIGHT.		HIGHEST WEIGHT.		AVERAGE WEIGHT.	
		8lbs.	0ozs.	8lbs.	0ozs.	8lbs.	0ozs.
1 Month.	1	8lbs.	0ozs.	8lbs.	0ozs.	8lbs.	0ozs.
2 ,,	7	7	12	12	4	8	2
3 ,,	20	6	10	25	0	14	2
4 ,,	8	4	0	13	2	9	0
5 ,,	7	4	10	38	0	13	8
6 ,,	3	7	14	22	8	13	0
7 ,,	4	7	8	13	8	11	1
8 ,,	3	12	5	14	6	13	3
9 ,,	1	12	8	12	8	12	8
10 ,,	2	11	4	20	0	15	15
11 ,,	4	10	0	13	0	12	1
12 ,,	7	10	0	17	10	15	0
13 ,,	7	10	0	16	8	12	9
14 ,,	15	7	2	22	0	14	1
15 ,,	4	17	0	18	14	17	4
16 ,,	15	8	0	22	0	15	3
17 ,,	4	12	10	14	0	12	13
18 ,,	8	14	0	28	0	15	8
19 ,,	3	13	4	19	8	16	4
20 ,,	5	14	0	23	6	17	0
21 ,,	2	11	8	11	10	11	5
22 ,,	2	13	0	15	0	14	0
23 ,,	None.						
2 Years.	26	12	0	26	0	17	12
3 ,,	21	15	4	39	12	24	0
4 ,,	14	18	0	36	0	27	8
5 ,,	14	23	8	44	8	29	2
6 ,,	9	21	0	39	6	21	6
7 ,,	13	29	0	51	0	34	1
8 ,,	1	40	0	40	0	40	0
9 ,,	9	35	12	46	8	38	6
10 ,,	6	40	0	56	0	45	2
13 ,,	5	54	0	69	8	57	4

An average child at birth should weigh 8lbs.

,,	,,	1 year	,,	24
,,	,,	6 years	,,	48
,,	,,	13 years	,,	82

BALLADE OF THE DREAM.

BY ANDREW LANG.

Swift as sound of music fled
  When no more the organ sighs.
Sped as all old joys are sped,
  So your lips, Love, and your eyes,
  So your gentle-voiced replies,
Mine, one hour, in sleep that seem,
  Flit away as slumber flies,
Following darkness like a dream.

As the scent from roses red,
  As the dawn from April skies,
As the phantom of the Dead,
  From the living love that hies,
  As the shifting shade that lies
On the moonlight-silvered stream,
  So you rise, when dreams arise,
Following darkness like a dream.

E

Could some witch, with woven tread,
 Could some spell in fairy wise,
Lap about this dreaming head
 In a mist of memories,
 I would lie like him that lies
Where the lights on Latmos gleam
 'Neath Selene down the skies
Following darkness like a dream.

ENVOY.

Sleep that grants what life denies,
Shadowy bounties and supreme,
 Bring me back the face, that flies
Following darkness like a dream.

THE BOY WHO FOLLOWED THE SUNSET.

BY MAY KENDALL.

THERE was a child who was small and frail, and could not understand the rough games of his comrades, but often spoiled their pleasure by his backwardness or timidity, so that they did not care to have him join them; and even if out of good-nature they let him share in their play, he was ridiculed for his awkward mistakes, and the more impatient boys called him careless and a spoilsport. Often this made him very unhappy, and at nights he used to pray that Heaven would make him brighter and stronger, like his playfellows; but this never came to pass. Indeed, his very longing for it stood in his way, and made him more apt to blunder, till by and by he was afraid to join in play at all, and would wander away by himself into quiet spots, and forget his failures in lonely dreaming. As he grew older this sensitiveness increased, and having no one (for

B 2

his mother had died when he was very young) to whom he could go for sympathy in his boyish troubles, the habit of solitary musing strengthened, and he loved to conjure up in his mind a place where all was different. He fancied himself strong and active, a king among his playfellows, or doing some great and heroic deed, and winning for himself great love and honour. But even in his dreams a restless discontent pursued him—a wish for something beyond life, some nameless and ineffable beauty that was hidden behind the beauty of the river and grass and hills. Most of all at sunset, when he watched the dying splendour of the sky, this feeling haunted him, and he longed to step out into the radiance and leave the earth behind. The land beyond the sunset became the home of all his dreams, and often he tried to reach it, but was always baffled by the falling night, and went home weary and disheartened. The glory of the sunrise he also thought an entrance into that distant country, though it never was so dear to him as the fading glory of the west; the rushing of water, and, more than all, the sound of music, were voices calling him far away.

There was one of his playmates more beautiful than the rest, whose face was like the faces he saw in dreams, and whose voice, when she sang, awakened the vague longings he could not understand. She mingled with the others; but he always felt a difference between them, and a reverence grew up in him for the child—the only one whose thoughts he could not guess, and who also loved to watch the sunset and the hills. Bertha was the swiftest and the readiest in all their play; yet she never laughed at his blunders as the others did, but helped him willingly and took his part. They all loved her, yet she was often alone, and many a time the boy saw her slight figure, with dark eyes and waving hair, flit by him in his solitary wanderings, till it became an interest with him to watch for her coming from some hidden nook, and a regret when the day passed and he had never seen her.

When he was yet young, his father died, and he was free to follow his old wish and seek the country beyond the sunset. There was little in the village that he should miss—only Bertha, and she was so much more bound up in his dreams with the beauty of the distant land than with the home where he had known her, that it hardly seemed to him he was leaving her behind in travelling towards the sunset. So one evening he set his face to the west, and walked till the sun sank, and then lay down to sleep. The next day he travelled on again, but when night fell the sunset country was yet distant, and night after night it seemed no nearer. Then the boy's heart grew weary, though he could not bear to give up hope and go back to his old home. Months went by, and even years, but the golden sunset was still beyond his reach, and he forgot the flowers and hills and glorious dawn in following it far away.

But one day, when the morning sun woke him from sleep, he knew that the time was not yet come to find the sunset country, and he turned and saw the domes of a great city glistening before him. Then, with a sigh, he set his face from the west and went towards the city, that lay on the shore of a great ocean. And there he found all the people working—some at ships, and some at marble, and some at metals; but none idle. All kinds of work were going on in this marvellous city. There were artists and musicians, under

whose hands sprang up wonderful shapes and sounds
of beauty; there were poets and philosophers, and
all had allotted them a certain share of labour, but
their common aim the boy could not understand.
As he looked, he saw that a place was also left for
him, with a portion of work, humble and simple as
he thought, for it was only carving in common wood.
But as he worked he saw that it was part of the
building of a great organ, and then he became better
content, and toiled on, though his hands grew tired,
and the sound of the waves breaking on the shore
still called him to that golden radiance he saw night
by night reflected on the sea. Often he thought his
work, though simple, ill and carelessly done, and
wearied of it, envying the players who should draw
glorious sounds from the keys at whose shaping he
had laboured. Yet the builder was satisfied, and the
organ grew into a beautiful and noble instrument,
worthy of a great musician.

At last, one day, he heard a voice singing, a voice
that he knew well. It was Bertha's, only stronger and
sweeter than in her childhood. Her share of the
work lay apart from his—only at rare intervals he

saw her, and saw that she was more beautiful than ever. He never spoke to her, and one day, at sunset, he missed her voice, and her place was filled by another. But it was to him as if she were still there, for her face and her singing haunted him constantly as he worked, and he knew at last that he never could forget them. Then more and more it seemed, at evening, that all the light and music and wonder of the city were but reflections from beyond the sunset sky, and that the beauty from which he might part with sorrow, if he could gain that country, would meet him again in greater radiance, and raise him up into its life.

Year by year the faces round him changed, and many new workers replaced the old ones, while the ocean glittered with ships that came and went, bearing passengers to and from the city. One day the builder of the organ embarked and left the shore, and his was almost the last of the old faces that had been familiar to the boy who entered the city—now so many years ago. Still he worked on, but now his work was nearly ended.

One evening, when the sky was radiant with sunset, the last stroke was added to his carving, and the tools dropped from his hands. Was he dreaming or awake? The glory of the sky was gathering round him, and he saw a path of gold leading across the water to the setting sun. A boat was by the shore, and as he entered it some power, whether wind or tide, floated it gently away along the gleaming track. The waves rippled about the keel, and it seemed as if low organ harmonies were blended with their tones. The path of gold deepened, narrowed, into the very heart of that ineffable splendour. . . . A cry broke from his lips, and the boat floated swiftly on; but those on shore could see it no longer, for their eyes were blinded by the glory.

KNURR AND SPELL.

BY WALTER POLLOCK.

CHAPTER I.

Mr. TUTTUTSON, the analytical dyer, was a man in whom a modest confidence was oddly blended with an ostentatious delight in his inventive successes. He was indeed a man in whom a freakish nature, departing from the usual custom of a dyer's hand growing to that it works in, had fitted the new man with a new characteristic, and had with feeble waggishness predestined the name for the bearer. For in his seeming moments of leisure, when he sat back with his eyes closed, a posture and face invariably adopted by thinkers for the purpose of thinking, he was wont to indulge in a favourite exclamation.

His nearest, in some sense his only, friend was an office clerk, suspected by some men of the world of being a Potentate in disguise, who, as all things in nature save the intangible have a name, was called

Toby Trimmer. It was their habit to meet often, to
talk often, and that loud and much, and generally
both at the same time and on different subjects.
This added to the liveliness of the discourse, and
eschewed the monotony of argument. But even to
the shining of the sun there are exceptions (when
eclipses happen, a point not always observed), and it
chanced that such an exception came when one day
their haphazard footsteps—which, however chancy,
always kept " time, time, time, in a sort of Runic
rhyme "—led them to a magnificent edifice devoted to
a vulgar purpose ; a huge and gilded chamber where
men met or parted, for the two actions are not
simultaneous, to eat and drink.

The dyer, who had closed his eyes and said, " Tut,
tut ! " while his keener companion had kept his on a
responsive satellite at a neighbouring bar, presently
left off thinking and spoke.

" Toby," he whispered rather than said, " I have
been in this place before."

" You tell me," said the other with a wide look,
" strange things."

" You will find them," replied the dyer hotly, " as

true as strange ; and that in these days is no light matter."

The tone, rather than the speech, recalled the clerk to matter-of-factness, and he asked quite simply :

"When, where, how, what, why, who?"

"You demand too much at once," said the dyer, with a dye—I mean a dry—smile. "But I will tell you this much to feed and whet your curiosity. It was not to-day, nor yesterday."

"Indeed!" answered the clerk, beating down his comrade with the airs of a man of fashion. "Who is she?"

"You might have surmised," said the dyer, "from the openness with which I broached so important a matter, that there was no she in the case."

"That," retorted the clerk, with a nettled twist of the mouth, "is as may be. Either way it alters the case."

"Now," said the dyer, "you speak like a lad of sense, and, believe me, I do not value your spirit one whit less than your intelligence. It was out of sight of my experience the most fanciful incident I have seen, though it may turn out to prove nothing in the telling."

"That," said the other, "I can well believe, both from hearsay and knowledge. But pray take me with you," he added, courteously waving off his companion's growing distrust of his interest.

"Well," resumed the dyer, "you will know, as a man of the world, that I am not bound to give you exact dates. But it was during my lifetime."

The other nodded gravely.

" I was sitting in this room, at this table, when two men came in with a certain dejected look, and took up a position at the adjoining one. I find it difficult to describe, with any certainty of being intelligible, the impression they produced on me, but this I can tell you, that they had so much the same air and haviour of haggardness and fatigue, that, but for their being entirely unlike in height, voice, colouring and figure, you might have taken them to be one and the same person."

" A strange reversal," muttered the clerk, "of the ordinary effect."

" I had not the honour, sir," said the dyer, who had heard him perfectly, "to catch your last remark."

" All right, old chap," began the clerk ; and then,

remembering his duty to the author, corrected himself thus : " It is, I think, to your advantage that you
did not ; for it was, I protest, a trivial interruption.
Your story interests me strangely. Proceed."

" These two men," added the dyer, " called each of
them, but in different voices, for a brandy-and-soda."

" For a brandy-and-soda ? and in different voices ?
Ay, ay !" said the clerk. " This begins to assume a
very different look. Can you, with due regard to
discretion, give me any information as to the appearance of these two men ?"

" I have told you," replied the other testily, " that
they were not the same. That for a legal clerk should
be enough."

" In some cases I do not say—but in an issue of
this moment—was one, for instance, short and the other
tall ?"

" You are right," said the other, whose astonishment
made him look for an instant like a man danced off his
fixity of tenure.

" Then," replied the clerk, " it may be, Master
Dyer, that I know your two men. Did they hold any
conversation ?"

"I will tell you," said the dyer, greatly impressed with his younger friend's sudden acuteness, "as nearly as I can remember, their own words."

CHAPTER II.

IT will perhaps be more convenient to give the narrative of what the dyer overheard in an unbroken course, shaping together at the end of it such irrelevant and interjectional remarks as we may see fit to attribute to the dyer, or the clerk, or both, or anybody else ; for it doesn't much matter.

The two men, then, at the adjoining table, had called each for his cup of brandy-and-soda, and when, with a dexterous circuit, the waiter had brought them what they desired, each sat sipping and eyeing the other with a curious look.

In saying that one was tall and the other short, the dyer had lied—it was a way he had got, for lying and dyeing differ only by two letters—but it was true that the two were in other ways unlike enough. They were of much the same height, but one, the elder of the two, a dark man, had a vast frame, which carried off (or, to speak by the card, carried on it) a certain tendency to portliness. The other did not resemble him in any of these points. Nor, being some years his junior, was he of the same age. The elder man bore in his visage and port all the signs of a country life, and a clever observer would therefore have said that he habitually lived in the country. This, again, was not the case with his companion.

"Snowle," said the younger presently, "I do not believe that this is a good kind of drink."

"How so?" asked the other.

"Partly," rejoined Montagu, "because I do not wish to compass the end which Falstaff assigned to sighing and grief, when he declared that they blew a man up like a bladder."

"Montagu," said Snowle, with a ring of sincerity, "I believe you are right there. Look at your French-man, who, whatever his faults may be—and I fancy we are pretty well agreed upon them—at any rate has a shrewd notion of taking care of his interior. Do you ever see *him* filling himself up with soda and brandy? Not he. He is far too wise. If he takes brandy, it is with his coffee, or without his coffee in a *petit verre.*"

"Quite so," Montagu assented; "but here in England we have come upon what a favourite dramatist of mine has termed the brandy-and-sodaic age, and in that I see excuse for the blue-ribbonites, who, however, I confess, do not please me much. I have known one of them seated at my own table, when I had provided him with all kinds of temperance drinks, descant for an hour by Shrewsbury clock to the assembled guests on their viciousness in drinking wine. And it was good wine, too," he added pathetically.

"Then," said Snowle, "he spoke, consciously or not, with the voice of envy."

"He spoke with a singularly tiresome voice," said Montagu. "But all this leads us away from my original proposition."

"Which is the converse," answered Snowle, "of the saying that all roads lead to Rome."

"You speak," cried Montagu admiringly, "like a man in a book."

"That," said Snowle, with a grave smile, "is because I am one. You will understand more of

C

these matters when you are as old as I am.   For the
present, enough said on that head.   You were saying ? " he added inquiringly.

"I was saying," rejoined Montagu, "long ago, and
should have repeated it longer ago if you had not
interrupted me—but, before we go further, may I ask
you, my oldest friend, one question ? "

"You may ask me," said Snowle, kindly as slowly,
"as many as you have time and both of us inclination
for.   Whether I shall answer or not is a question still
lying in the lap of the gods."

"Why do we both talk in the same manner and
phraseology, and both of them so very odd ? "

CHAPTER III.

"No more of this fooling," said Snowle, speaking
for the first time sternly.   "We are in a public place,
and as there are some fifty people sitting close by us,
it is barely possible that we may be observed."

"I had not thought of that," cried the other, "and
I assure you I regret what I have said."

"You are forgiven," said Snowle, with a stately inclination of the head ; "and we will now consider your original proposition, which was, if I mistake not——"

"That brandy-and-soda is an ill drink. I will go further, and say that, to me at least, spirits in any form are harmful rather than advantageous."

"It may be so," rejoined Snowle ; and casting a look of pride at his own massive proportions, as though to prefer them to his companion's slighter build, he added, "I will tell you what I will do. I will make a compact with you."

Then, leaning forward, he spoke rapidly and in a low tone some words, of which the listener, Mr. Tut-tutson, could only distinguish the following:

"Till we meet again—great strait—Redhill—is it agreed?"

"One moment," said Montagu, in doubtful tones. "What did we do this time three days ago three years ago?"

In spite of the inward form of the question, Snowle replied like a man who had learnt a lesson by rote :

"We went to see a performance of 'The Corsican

C 2

Brothers.' It occurs to me that a mysterious sympathy of that kind, if it grew up in our cases, might be inconvenient.

"Nonsense, boy!" said the other. "You have been reading novels of occultism and shilling tales of wonder."

"On the contrary, I have been reading———"

Here the younger man leant across the table with a communicative whisper, which the listener failed to catch. But thereafter he asserted that the two shook hands and got up. Then the younger made a show of paying for what they had had, but allowed himself to be easily over-persuaded by the elder. Then they walked out, each wearing a satisfied smile. And the narrator further insisted that, in spite of the mysterious reference to "The Corsican Brothers," they were still quite different.

"And now," said Mr. Tuttutson to Toby, "what do you think of it?"

Toby, who during the narrative had put in here and there a pertinent question with a disengaged, even a double-and-disengaged, air, replied deliberately:

" I think I can guess who your Snowle is. As to the other, I can but conjecture. But it is very plain to me that something passed between these two men."

At this expanse of legal acumen the dyer could only stare. The clerk saw his advantage, and pressed it.

" I shall make it my business," he said sturdily, " as it will also be my pleasure, to unravel this sleave. I shall fit the cap upon your younger interlocutor. In fact, if his name is Montagu, mine shall be Cap — you—let."

CHAPTER IV.

IT was Snowle's habit, simple as his rural tastes were, to keep a modest *pied-à-terre* in London, and, in order to avoid attracting attention, he had chosen for this purpose a disused luncheon and drinking bar in a small street in one of the most crowded parts of the town. It was on the ground-floor, and he had furnished it by, in the first instance, simply reversing the modern order of things, and having plates on the table instead of on the wall.

One night, not long after the events just narrated, two footmen (I do not mean lackeys, but persons who are footmen as opposed to horsemen) might have been seen wending their way towards this place, had anyone observed them. And, as though to prove that fiction is sometimes quite as commonplace as truth, out of the hurrying crowd which thronged the streets some one did observe them. This was a person so elaborately disguised as a retired Indian colonel, that no one could possibly help at once discerning that he was a clerk. He had in one pocket "M. Lecoq," and in another—for there was not room for both volumes in the same—"Le Crime de l'Opera." These he would from time to time pull out and study with air of comparative philosophy by the light of a street lamp, never, however, losing sight of the two whom he seemed to be shadowing. How he accomplished this feat is a matter which need not be explained. He followed them in this manner to the Deserted Restaurant, and was then compelled to relinquish his quest for a time, because, having opened the portal and gone in, they closed it behind them. He felt like a man in whose face a door had been suddenly shut. We may take a privilege which was not his (because he did not write this story), and overhear the conversation which took place between them.

" You bet——" said Snowle.

"An American phrase, I think," sighed Montagu.

"Not at all," said Snowle, with a peremptory nod, " I was about to say, you bet that within the time stated our compact is broken, and that one or both of us will suffer heavily for it in an unforeseen way."

" I do," said Montagu calmly. " I know it, for I have been reading—— "

CHAPTER V.

At this moment there was a violent knocking at the door, which Snowle opened, so that it was possible to see what was outside it. This was apparently a waiter from a neighbouring tavern, carrying a tray supporting bottles of soda-water and other things such as a waiter might be expected to carry on a tray. (It is not for nothing that a person reads Gaboriau and Boisgobey.)

"You sent for this, gentlemen?" asked the waiter in a tone halting between hope and mistrust.

"I," replied Montagu, who being the youngest, naturally spoke first, "have given no such command."

"And," added Snowle, with a jolly laugh, "nothing was nearer my thoughts or further from my intentions. Ho, ho !"

"My good friend," added Montagu, in silvery yet menacing tones, "there is clearly some unfortunate mistake. It would be better to—— "

"Go before you kick me out," interrupted the waiter, with swift apprehension. "Yes, sir. Certainly, sir !"

And therewith he vanished.

"He looked like a waiter," said Snowle thoughtfully.

"You remind me," replied Montagu, "of the naturalists who first discovered the skunk—not that I mean to compare an excellent and deserving class of men with a beautiful but disagreeable animal."

" I am not acquainted with the story," said Snowle proudly.

" Then," replied Montagu, seizing his opportunity, "you shall be. The following observations passed between them : ' It looks like a skunk—it smells like a skunk—it behaves like a skunk. Let's call it a skunk.' "

"This," replied Snowle, his voice taking a sonorous ring, " is trifling. Montagu, *that* is *no* waiter ! "

" What ! " said the other ; "not a Knight-Temp— "

"No ! " thundered Snowle. " Did you ever know me make hackneyed quotations, save from my own immortal works ? No, boy ; no waiter, but a masquerading clerk."

Montagu stood open-mouthed at his friend's sagacity. He had had many proofs of it from Snowle's frequently calling him a fool, but it always struck him with a keen and over-mastering surprise.

" How—how," he muttered falteringly " did you discover this ? "

(It never occurred to him to doubt a fact thus announced by a man who said he was the cleverer of the two.)

"Oh," replied Snowle, with a smile of fine scorn hovering on his upper lip, "do you mean that you did not see?"

"No! What? Tell me!"

"I will; but I will tell you first why you should not thus have failed in observation."

"Oh, mercy!" groaned Montagu; "more talkee-talkee! I mean," he added, correcting himself, "I shall be happy to listen to any information you may be pleased to give me."

"Then," returned Snowle, with a gratified face, "you shall observe that it is a maxim with detectives in novels that a criminal always forgets some trifling matter, which in the end gives a clue to his detection. This may also occur to persons who assume disguises, and you may here observe that, both in actual life and in novels, criminals sometimes have become detectives. This was so with Vidocq and with Gaboriau's Lecoq."

"He told quite another story about him in another novel," said Montagu feebly.

"Boy!" cried Snowle loudly; "let *me* tell *my* story. I am not in a position to state why the person who has just left us assumed a disguise. But of this I am certain, that he is not a waiter, but a clerk. He had forgotten a detail which none but a practised eye could seize. He had——"

"What?" cried Montagu, roused to an agony of questioning.

"*A pen behind his ear!*"

· · · ———— · ·

CHAPTER VI.

"There is something in that," said Montagu.

"Say the word again," said Snowle, "and I will drive this dagger to your heart."

"You quote Lever," rejoined Montagu, "and Archimedes had none."

"None what?" asked Snowle in a secret voice, for he saw that the quondam waiter, disguised as a Swiss field-marshal, was listening at the key-hole.

"None Powstow," said Montagu, at once catching his older friend's meaning.

"Powstow!" said the supposed field-marshal to

himself; " that, then, is the name of a third accomplice."

And therewith he hurried off to convey this intelligence to his older friend, concealing the fact that he was disguised by picking up and putting on two sandwich-boards, which he had left ready at the nearest corner.

Meanwhile, Snowle and Montagu interchanged a last grip of the hand, and so parted, Montagu softly murmuring " The Compact "; and Snowle sending out in a stentorian voice the words, " The Compact ! Ho! Ho!"

Toby had given an old apple-woman, who, unbeknown to him, was one of the greatest of living French detectives, a sum of money to see where the two friends went, and he learnt in due course that Snowle had taken a ticket for Northgate-on-Sea (a place to which he went because he lived there), and that Montagu had returned to his London lodging.

But the first remarkable thing that came of the two friends' strange meeting, Toby was not privileged to witness.

One of Montagu's attractions was a certain largeness of sentiment (art-critics speak of a large feeling, and they must be right), which at this period had led him into a particularity of affection.

It was a very few days after he had parted from Snowle that he went to call on the mother of Miss Cantilene, a young lady for whom he cherished the tenderest feelings. He was fortunate in getting an opportunity of speaking alone with her, and he was not inapt to lead their conversation to a point which enabled him to hint at the emotions which possessed him.

"*Miss Cantilene*," he had said, after an eloquent, if vague, appeal, which he meant to be received with favour, "*what I mean is this: I have learned to long for your society, your presence, to remember and to dream over your lightest words, to consider them, to weigh them this way and that, in the wild hope of finding in them the meaning which I should wish to find. I think, indeed, of nothing else. Could but I hope that my aspirations are not entirely vain; could you but give me*——." Here he stopped dead short, and a strange and horrible expression passed over his face. He collected himself, and resumed: "*Could you but give me——.*" Again the spasm seized him, and in a dull voice, and with wide-staring eyes, he continued : " *Could you but give me—a glass of brandy ?* "—adding in heart-broken accents, and more than half to himself : " The fellow's drinking soda-water, confound him ! "

Miss Cantilene looked at him in amaze, and said with quiet dignity :

" Mr. Montagu, I fear you are not quite yourself."

" That," he replied sadly, "is unluckily a great deal truer than you think it is. Pray, pray, forgive me, and make my excuses to your mother. It is a mystery—I cannot explain now. Some day it may be possible. Once more, forgive me ! " and with these words he fled, leaving the girl whom he adored, angry, astonished, and puzzled.

Montagu got into a cab in a state of misery, was driven to his club in a state of misery, ordered a liqueur-glass of brandy in a state of misery, and, having drank it, sat down and reflected.

" It is just like Snowle," he said to himself ; " he has got thirsty and forgotten all about it, and probably ruined all my hopes with Miss Cantilene. In such a case as this I will have revenge, even on my oldest and dearest friend. I'll go home and dine ; this time *I* will drink soda-water."

He did ; with vast perseverance and discomfort he got through half a dozen bottles of soda-water, and then went wretchedly to bed, wondering what would come of it. What did come of it was this : Snowle, while Montagu was dining alone and wretched in his London lodgings, was playing billiards at Northgate, in a friend's house. The friend presently suggested to him a brandy-and-soda, the materials for mixing which stood on a side-table.

"No, thank you," replied Snowle. "I mustn't touch it ; it's against my—my doctor's orders." ·

"Doctor's orders ? " said the friend ; I never knew you had a doctor ; you certainly have never wanted one."

"Well, no," replied Snowle somewhat confusedly ; "but you see, the fact is that——" Here he suddenly made a wry face, such as a man makes who absently helps himself to ice pudding, not having observed the nature of the *plat*. "Confound the boy ! " he said, irrelevantly, as it seemed to his friend. "I'll change my mind, please, and have a liqueur

glass of brandy by itself." This he poured out and
drank, and then said, again as it seemed to his friend
with some irrelevance, " So, Master Montagu, now I
know what to expect."

Before the three games of billiards they had agreed
to play were finished, Snowle had quietly drunk six
liqueur-glasses of old cognac, which interfered neither
with his play nor with his comfort, after which he
went home to bed, and waked the next morning as
well as possible just at the same time when Montagu
waked from a series of nightmares, in many of which
he had figured as a balloon.

CHAPTER VII.

THE next incident in the double, yet strangely united,
life of the two friends, shall be given as it was recounted
to Mr. Tuttutson by Toby, who, again disguised,
appeared as a hired waiter at a dinner given by
Montagu's rich uncle and godfather, Mr. Goodlad, in
honour of Montagu's birthday.

" Mr. Tuttutson," said Toby Trimmer.

" Toby Trimmer," said Mr. Tuttutson.

" Mr. Tuttutson," said Toby Trimmer.

" Toby Trimmer," said Mr. Tuttutson.

" Look here, old chap," rejoined Toby, " when I went in for this game I bargained, mentally or otherwise, for talking like people in books. *But*——"

" Well? " said the dyer.

" Well? " said Toby, from a vile habit, which he instantly repudiated by adding, " You have caught me tripping once again, but never no more. You have tried me much, and I have never yet appealed. But —here I take my stand (an American expression, you will observe)—I will NOT talk Howells."

" Your answer," replied the dyer, " interests, but does not surprise me. Proceed."

" May I talk like a man out of a book? " queried Toby timidly.

" I wish to heaven you *were* a man out of *this* book," replied the dyer, and then put as a semicolon to his remark, " At least, I should do so were I an unbiased critic, unconnected (as I wish I were) with any literary loves or hatreds. I should add," he said, with a wise suddenness, "that I have no control over your speech, since I share your invidious position."

"O. K.," said Toby with an eponymous wink, and then in his turn added, "I mean, all shall be done as you please. These, sir, are the facts. I waited——"

" You might have waited longer, for all I cared," said the dyer.

"I waited," resumed Toby, disregarding the inter ruption, which, if regarded, might have injured the narration, "I waited disguised as a waiter, at Mr Goodlad's dinner. Mr. Montagu came in."

" When did he go out?" asked Tuttutson thought-lessly.

" After he had come in," replied Toby. "Let me now be brief."

" You *shall*," rejoined the dyer ; and added, with the air of a man breaking a confidence to himself, " that will please the public."

" Public?" said Toby, catching his last word. "Not at all. It was at Mr. Goodlad's. I was there, as I told you, in disguise. I know some gay actors, and they gave me the tip. I had a gauze neck, *papier-mâché* toes, and——"

" It were tedious to go o'er," said the dyer; "and now, do drop style and come to facts."

Toby straightened himself up, and said all in one breath, save when nature, resenting police interference, compelled him to take breath at a most inappropriate moment :

" From information received, waited, as a waiter, at Mr. Goodlad's on Wednesday last. Dinner-party. Mr. Montagu present as guest. While soup was being served, Mr. Montagu turned pale and called for brandy. Butler—discreet person—whispered, " Master's finest old dry sherry." Mr. Montagu persisted—said, " Damn all sherry ! Brandy it is. He's drinking soda." Servants were puzzled. Mr. Goodlad was annoyed. Brandy was given to him as per request. Later on, Mr. Goodlad produced (this was after the ladies had gone up to the drawing-room) some—as he said, and as I know——"

" How do you know ? " asked the dyer.

" As I know," continued Toby, without moving a muscle — "some exquisite Bordeaux. This was offered to Mr. Montagu. He was about to raise a glass containing this nectar to his lips, when he fell back in his chair and cried out with offensive loudness, '*Soda-water!*' 'Soda-water?' asked Mr. Goodlad, with grave insistence; 'it is old wine.' 'Yes,' returned Montagu, 'it is, but it will be older to-morrow; you cannot deny that. Oh! what am I saying?' he added. 'It's here—it's here—he's at it.' 'At what?' asked the host. 'At—at—atavis edite regibus—regibus or omnibus—tous les chats sont gris le soir—Buona notte, M. Atavis—bon soir, Signor Grislesoir—gute nacht, Herr Pantaleone—Now —maintenant—nun—jam (not currant but elegiacs)— dans this augenblick—ci—he's drinking cognac—he's been reading About and Besant. Take me away— any way—out of this!' With these wild words," Toby concluded, "he was carried forth, and that night I saw him no more."

"You have given me," said the dyer, "much to think over."

"Then," rejoined Toby, "I had better light the candles."

"By no means," said the dyer benignantly. "I would have you to remember that I always think best in bed. I am going to bed. Man," he continued, while his eyes danced with sleep, "I am an excellent thinker."

"Thinker, thailor, soldier, sailor," began Toby feebly, and then, with an unexpected bow, lighted his patron out of the room.

CHAPTER VIII.

LEFT alone, the clerk struck his clenched hand with his open forehead several times, and then betook himself to Montagu's residence.

The policeman on the beat was his third cousin, and in his company he walked up and down until the early morning, when Montagu, pale and dishevelled, appeared upon the doorstep, muttering.

Toby, if he had had six ears, would have used them all to listen. He had only two, and these he employed.

"Redhill," he heard Montagu say. "It certainly must be so. I will telegraph before I start, and Snowle will—nay, he shall meet me there." The speaker had closed the street-door in a fit of abstraction, and now he rang at it to summon a maid. "Mary," he said, when she appeared. I shall not be home till dinner-time. I am going to—into the country."

"But, sir," said Mary wonderingly, "you've still got your dress-clothes on!"

"No matter," said Montagu drearily, "*he* hasn't."

"And I beg your pardon, sir," said Mary, "but it's raining, and you've only taken a stick."

"No matter," again said Montagu fatally, "*he* has his umbrella;" and with this he started for the railway-station in a hansom.

CHAPTER IX.

TOBY, following him in another hansom, altered the arrangements of his reversible ulster so that it looked like a cassock, made himself up with a few sticks of *crayon gras* and a hand-glass, discharged the cab at the corner before the station, and, following close on

Montagu's heels, took his ticket in a Curatic fashion for Redhill. He was so absorbed in the change that he scarcely noticed a person who seemed, with offensive obviousness, to be a Railway Director, and who stumbled against him in his eagerness to secure a ticket for Portsmouth by the same train which was to carry Montagu and Toby to Redhill.

Montagu got out at Redhill.

So did Toby.

So did the Railway Director.

Montagu went straight to the refreshment-room.

So did Toby.

So did the Railway Director.

Montagu was met by a large, jovial, well-looking man.

"Why, damme," said Toby, surprised into speaking half aloud, "that's the other one!"

"Oh, oh, oh!" said the obvious Railway Director to himself with three different intonations; "then this, as I thought, is no Curate; and now I have them all."

"Snowle," said Montagu pathetically, in an undertone of which not a syllable was lost by the clerk and the Director, "see what you have made of me!"

"Ho! ho!" laughed Snowle, and his laughter seemed to shake the station. "You would have it so, boy. But, indeed, I am of opinion that it has gone far enough. Waiter! two brandies-and-sodas!

The two friends drank the two brandies-and-sodas in solemn silence. The effect upon Montagu was remarkable. He grew suddenly cheerful, and proceeded to relate to his elder friend (at great length) all that had happened since their parting.

Toby, hunched up in a corner with a Bath bun, listened with growing astonishment. When Montagu had finished, he rose, and said to himself: "So that's it. When one drank soda, the other was to drink brandy. When the other drank brandy, the one was to drink soda. Strange—but I must hurry to tell my patron."

He was about to leave the refreshment-room, when the Director stopped him quietly but in a masterful manner, saying, with a slight foreign accent:

"So this is how we avoid our old friends?"

"Old friends?" said Toby, aghast.

"Surely," replied the Director, "you have not forgotten Pâlot, of the Sûreté? It is for that little forgery I want you—the extradition warrant is all in order."

" O Lord !" said Toby, and collapsed.

Before he had come to himself enough to convince the French detective that he had made a mistake, the two friends had disappeared.

The Frenchman, however, was equal to the occasion. Like all good policemen he had a clue, and, armed with this weapon, he and Toby followed Snowle and Montagu to the house of the Cantilenes, where, by a happy chance, the dyer happened to be calling.

Montagu then, for the second time, related (again at great length) all that had happened.

Miss Cantilene accepted the explanation, and him.

The dyer gave a learned address, and took Montagu into partnership.

Toby became a variety entertainer.

Pâlot returned to Paris, and wrote an article for the *Figaro*, explaining, with illustrations, that in England all clerks are amateur detectives of great skill in disguise.

Snowle laughed, and went back to his country-house.

A MACHINE HAND.

(LONDON, E.C.)

BY T. ASHE.

My little milliner has slipp'd
   The doctors, with their drugs and ways:
Her years were only twenty-two,
   Though long enough her working days.

She went at eight through wet and snow,
   Nor dallied for the sun to shine,
And walked an hour to work and home,
   Content if she was in by nine.

She had a little gloomy room,
   Up stair on stair, within the roof,
Where hung her pictures on the wall,
   Wherever it was weather-proof.

She held her head erect and proud,
   Nor asked of man or woman aid ;

And struggled till the last ; and died
   But of the parish pit afraid.

Jennie, lie still ! the hair you loved
   You wraps, unclipped, if you but knew !
We by a quiet graveyard wall,
   For love and pity, buried you !

THE CHIPPENDALE CHAIR.

BY E. M. ABDY-WILLIAMS (*Mrs. Bernhard Whishaw*).

It was not a settle, nor yet a couch,
But a double Chippendale chair,
And it filled the whole of the window wide,
In the curtained corner there.
And the lady sat with her gown spread out,
And a frown on her face so fair,
While the gallant prayed she would but make room
For two on the Chippendale chair.

The lady sat with her gown spread out,
And the galiant, he stood beside,
And he twirled a ring with a diamond stone
And muttered and stuttered and sighed,
Till she rose with a bend of her haughty head,
And made him a curtsey rare,
And he bowed himself out of the dim recess
Where stood the Chippendale chair.

But there came another, in humbler mood,
  Who offered nor wealth nor gold,
Save the wealth of worship his eyes confessed,
  And the boundless love they told.
And then the lady drew back her gown
  With a blush on her face so fair,
And they found there was plenty of room for two
  On the quaint old Chippendale chair.

HOW I PAID HALF-A-CROWN TO SEE "TRYING A MAGISTRATE."

BY J. L. TOOLE.

"I don't think I want a ticket," I said to the lady at the door.

"And why not?" she asked.

"I am Mr. Toole," I said, smiling in my best manner.

"That will not do," she answered, smiling in what was evidently her worst.

"Won't do," I said, "why not?"

"You must pay, sir," she answered, with increased severity, "the tickets are half-a-crown."

"But I am going to recite for the charity," I said, not liking to be treated as an impostor.

"Oh, I dare say," she replied, and there was such an amount of what the dramatists call withering scorn in the expression of her face, that I felt further discussion might be awkward, for she was a very fine woman, and moreover, the time had arrived when I was to have been on the platform ; so I paid half-a-crown to hear myself recite, and, looking at the transaction from an auditor's point of view, I need not say I was very much delighted. I heard myself try a magistrate, and I don't mind telling you between ourselves (of course I should not like it to go any further) that I think it was one of the most amusing recitals I ever heard, so full of genuine wit, and yet so genial ; you feel while you hear it a certain amount of sympathy for the magistrate, and yet you cannot help laughing at him. If he had not been a particularly kind-hearted magistrate he would certainly have committed that witness for contempt of court—I know I should have done so.

By the way, did you ever hear of the American who stepped into a Massachusetts court one day, and spent some time in hearing the trials. Presently a man was brought up for contempt of court and fined, whereupon the stranger rose from his seat and advancing to the bar, said, " How much was the defendant fined ? "

" Five dollars," replied the usher.

" Well, if that's all, I'd like to jine in," and he laid

down five dollars, saying, " I have had a few hours'
experience of this court, and no one can feel a greater
contempt for it than I do, and I am willing to pay
for it ! "

You can pay for almost anything in America.   But
I was telling you about the Charity Bazaar where I
paid to see myself, and when I come to think of it, I
never spent half-a-crown to better advantage, so much
so, that when the lady at the door offered me her
apologies and that half-crown back again I refused
both.   " My dear lady," I said, " I have enjoyed the
entertainment very much.   I think Mr. Toole is worth
double the money ;   and whenever he comes to
Blunderford again, I hope you will let me know."

She said she hoped I would let her know, she had
never been so much annoyed at herself in all her life ;
but she was very glad to inform me that I was not the
only one by hundreds who had paid to see me Trying
a Magistrate, which had resulted in a large addition to
the Hospital Fund.   She confessed I had tried her
too, but she did not mind if I didn't.   " To tell you
the truth," she said, " I thought I should have dropped
when I saw you come on the stage, and you were Mr.

Toole after all." (The audience were differently affected, I am glad to say.) In the language of the immortal Bard, I remarked, "All's well, that ends well"; in her own equally familiar vernacular, she replied, "That's true." And so we parted, both of us a trifle wiser than when first we met, but neither of us the sadder for our pleasant interchange of incivilities.

QUEEN VICTORIA'S DAY.

An Ode on the 50th Anniversary of her Reign.

BY THOS. GORDON HAKE.

AVANT COURIER.

Statecraft and kingly power for ages schooled
The nation's will; the rod of genius ruled;
At last, glad day, a maiden's gentle hand
Sufficed to guide the reins of State by sea and land.
Then said a voice from Heaven, her lengthened reign
Is to eclipse the pride of kings:
A virgin Queen has come again,
And to all loving homes her blessing brings.
Soon this Queen shall be a bride,
And with her faithful Prince her State divide,
His virtues matched by hers alone,
A fitting glory to her throne.
So shall their perfect lives be blest
Till Heaven, who knows our welfare best,
Calls him the earliest to his rest.

Since hath the gracious sun

Fifty times his year begun,

And she remains, our hope and hourly care,

Her children round her, many a happy pair !

England, be this a day of mirth

From dawn to utmost even !

It is a day to keep on earth ;

The day is kept in heaven.

Partake the wine and break the bread :

This day shall all her poor be fed.

There is joy o'er the blessings her reign has showered

down,

Yet lone is the star that shines in her crown.

Though sickness and sorrow are common to all,

In our joy let our hearts the departed recall ;

Let us think of the friend

In her youth so beloved :

May our blessing attend

On his home far removed !

His name, held so dear, to our children be told ;

He loved her, revered her, in days that are old,

He blesses her still her children among,

For the days that are old are the days that were young.

Oh, the days of our youth, what memories they fill !
We looked on her then and we look on her still.
Who now blind once beheld her, to her are not blind,
They treasure their Queen in their innermost mind :
Who deaf once gave ear to the tones of her voice,
Remember them still, in her accents rejoice.

CHORUS.

Since hath the gracious sun
Fifty times his year begun,
And she remains, our hope and hourly care,
Her children round her, many a happy pair !

England, be this a day of mirth
From dawn to utmost even ;
It is a day to keep on earth,—
The day is kept in heaven.

Rejoice the heart from labour free,
It is a holy Jubilee !
Where grief does not sadden
Let mirth the heart gladden ;
Where our wanderings have been,
Where our footsteps may stray,

Remember the Queen
  On her Jubilee day.
Rejoice, O brave legions,
In the sun-gilded regions!
  There reigns she afar.
Rejoice, O brave souls,
At the furthermost poles !
  Her children ye are.

May no grief her heart sadden,
May this day her heart gladden:
Victoria sits on her earth-rounded throne !
From the waters that freeze into mountains of stone
To the fire-flashing shores of the tropical zone.
When a soldier has fallen a tear can she shed,
With the widow she knows how to mourn for the
    dead ;
She makes all the cares of her kingdoms her own.
Though the touch of the monarch no longer heals,
As balm to the heart her sympathy steals.

  'Tis her own Jubilee !
  Where her ships plough the deep,

       Let no memories sleep ;
       Where the thunder hangs mute,
       Let her cannon salute
         Every wave of the sea.

   Musicians, whose glory it is to control
Our hearts and to sunder our cares from the soul,
Strike deep where hope's solace we seek for in vain,
Strike deep, though of ills hard to bear we complain !
Strike deep to the hearts of the soldiers who guard
The precincts of freedom, our love their reward ;
Strike chords that in battle their sufferings appease,
Till their banners seem floating in victory's breeze.

   It is summer, the June of the Jubilee year,
The month when the first-fruits of spring-time appear,
The month when the lark thrills the sky with a song,
Where the blue-bells hang silent the moorlands along.
It is June, glorious June, the month of the Queen !
The cornfields are paling, the pastures are green,
The ferns are uncurling, the hedge-rows are gay
With wild roses as welcome as blossom of May,
       The trees are swelled out
         In the foliage of spring,

The cuckoo's about
With its voice on the wing.

The morning has come, the churches pour forth
The battling of bells from the south to the north ;
The peals from the belfries are merrily rung,
All hearts are rejoicing, all nature is young.

The joys of the earth while they last are our own,
Let us give them to her, to her hearth, to her throne.
Victoria, loved Queen ! We proclaim thee again,
May the trust we repose ever sweeten thy reign !

Loud and deep are the cheers 'neath the old village
oak :
The health, the long life of the Queen they invoke.
A fife at the lips and a drum all their band,
The villagers gladden the length of the land :
The bunting from gable to gable is swung,
The casements with flags and fond mottoes are hung,
The maidens, alert from the burst of the morn,
Their bosoms with sweet-scented posies adorn :
In the love-threaded dance their steps are untired

As they weave them to tunes by affection inspired.

The children are shouting and romping in throngs :

Like anthems seem holy their merriest songs.

The wayfarer pauses in crossing the stile ;

He lists in a dream to their voices awhile :

The voices of children a stranger may win ;

Through them are our hearts with the angels akin.

'Twas so on the day she ascended the throne :

We live o'er again the days that are gone,

The days of our youth !   What memories they fill,—

We looked on her then and we look on her still !

GRAND CHORUS.

Victoria sits on her earth-rounded throne !

From the waters that freeze into mountains of stone

To the fire-flashing shores of the tropical zone,

> Her kingdoms are free !
> Where her ships plough the deep,
> Let no memories sleep ;
> Where the thunder hangs mute,
> Let her cannon salute
> Every wave of the sea.

Rejoice, O brave legions,
In the sun-gilded regions !
　There reigns she afar ;
Rejoice, hardy souls,
At the furthermost poles !
　Her children ye are.

THE TWO COTS.

BY C. CHESTON.

HUSHED silence reigns supreme; the lamp, turned low,
    Lights up a corner of the spacious room,
Where wife and husband, knit in common woe,
    Watch their child suffer in the darkening gloom.
The summer day dies hard; the heavy air,
    Unfreshened by the coolness of the night,
Breathes hotly o'er the infant lying there
    With flushing cheeks, and eyes unduly bright.
The quickened breath, the feeble ceaseless moan,
    Mute cry of pain from lips too young to speak,
Wring from the father's heart an answering groan,
    Send swift tears coursing down the mother's cheek.
It is her firstborn; born to high estate,
    To wealth beyond computing, to a name
Itself a priceless heritage, yet fate
    Hangs dubious o'er that fever-stricken frame.
Princes of science leave their graver cares
    To bring wise counsel in this lordling's need;

A skilful nurse the mother's vigil shares,

   Giving each slightest want the swiftest heed.

Ah! mother, watching with an anguished heart,

   Thine infant feebly struggling for its life,

Longing to set it free, and bear its part

   Of pain and suffering in the feverish strife :

Whose infinite nobility of love

   Would give up all, so that thy child might live,

Placing its mere existence far above

   All that wealth, station, or a name can give !

Cast but thine eye a hundred yards away

   From the broad square, where stands thy stately

      hall,

To the foul court, where grim despair holds sway,

   And poverty outspreads its funeral pall !

There, in yon attic, might thine eye discern

   A mother suffer pangs akin to thine,—

A wailing infant's lips with fever burn,

   Tended by love, like thine own heart's, divine—

Yet all around is changed, that slender purse,

   Drained every day for bread at hunger's call,

Can pay no doctor's fee, no watchful nurse :

   A mother's love must do the work of all !

The air that struggles through the propped-up frame
    Teems with ill odours, wafts on every breath
The drunken laugh that tells of cynic shame,
    The oaths and shouts of those who fight beneath.
By one poor candle's light, with aching head,
    With features wasted more with woe than age,
The worn out woman plies th' unceasing thread
    That feeds her children with its meagre wage.
Nor rests she, save with loving touch to smooth
    The ragged couch on which her babe is lain :
Or with angelic tenderness to soothe
    The restless movements of its silent pain :
Or just to glance where, stretched upon the floor
    On a thin pallet, other two lie still,
Hungry, yet taught they must not ask for more,
    But be good children, since their brother's ill.
See, as a staggering step ascends the stair,
    What silent terror glances in her eye,
The grateful lips find utterance in prayer
    As the dread terror for the time goes by !

      *   *   *   *   *

Enough ! a vulgar tale of common want,
    Of low-born refuse, and their hopes and fears :

Give up, I pray, this hypocritic cant
    Of sorrows quite unfit for cultured ears.
The workhouse is the place for such as these :
    There they can live at least from want removed—
The crime of giving alms just as we please
    Political economy has proved.

         *   *   *   *   *

Out ! comfortable cant of callous greed,
    That turns its back on sorrow, shame, and sin,
And spurns the deathless poet's kindlier creed,
    "One touch of nature makes the whole world kin !"
Preach as thou may'st, one heritage of care
    Binds man to man in ties thou canst not loose :
And of thy surplusage a fitting share
    Stands mortgaged to thy needing brother's use.
Spurn not the sacred duty, lest the curse
    Of outraged nature fall upon thy head,
For thee, as well as Crœsus, stands the verse,
    Call no man happy until he be dead.
Thank God ! to woman thou may'st prate in vain,
    Such dogmas find no echo in her breast ;
Swift to discern, prompt to allay the pain,
    She spurns her own, so she gives others rest.

Alone, amid this money-cursèd age
  Woman's self-sacrifice still gives to man
A holier instinct, as a sure presage
  Of life unfettered by this mortal span.
Thus maidens, highly nurtured, quit their ease,
  Stooping ?   Nay ! rising to the menial duty,
Striving with eager art the sick to please,
  Making each sufferer's cot a thing of beauty.
Ye Queens of Womanhood, earth holds no crown
  Meet for the brows of angels such as ye !
Sweet charity shall mark you for her own
  With heavenly light through all eternity !
Each grateful glance that greets your kindly love,
  Each timid whisper struggling to be bold
From suffering children, stores for you above
  Riches no earthly treasury can hold.

        *   *   *   *   *   *   *

Mothers ! whom closer ties forbid to roam
  In search of sorrows ye would fain assuage,
Whose love finds fitting duties nearer home,
  Think on the war with grief these women wage !
And, as your happy children round your knee
  (The sweetest picture to your loving eye)

Laugh at a fairy tale in happy glee,

 Unconscious of their fellows' misery :

Teach their young hearts to feel another's grief,

 Show them the purest joy they e'er can know

Is found in giving comfort and relief

 To those condemned to poverty and woe.

Tell them the rose that blooms upon the hedge

 Is cousin to the cultured hot-house flower :

Want is no crime, sickness no sacrilege

 That we should blame the paupers of the hour.

One power made us all, ease nurtures some

 In peaceful indolence to spend their time :

Want stifles others, till in time they come

 From youth neglected to an age of crime.

Each waif that struggles on its sordid path

 Hath yet a spark of nobleness within ;

Seize it, and turn it from the coming wrath

 That waits upon a life of shame and sin.

And for the sick ones : help the skilful band

 Of girls who labour in our Shadwell wards :

Their hero lives your sympathy commands :

 The work their strength is spent in is the Lord's.

A VICIOUS CIRCLE.

BY THE EARL OF LYTTON.

I.

How fleas are put to death we all know well,
But how they come to being who can tell ?
Long ere by Monsieur Pouchet it was stated,
The common people took for demonstrated
Without the need of any demonstration
The Doctrine of Spontaneous Generation ;
And they aver that fleas from sawdust come
All cap-a-pie, complete and mettlesome
As arm'd Minerva from Jove's brain, or free
As full-grown Aphrodite from the sea,
Or rising statesmen from the Cabinet
Into which no one guesses how they get.

II.

O Spallanzani, Spallanzani, fie !
How couldst thou circulate that heresy
Ex ovo omne vivum? Were it true,

Would not the world's end be too much ado

About an omelette?   But it matters not;

For no inch nearer truth wouldst thou have got.

If thou precisely the reverse hadst said,

Nor will "*ex vivo omne ovum*" aid

Our knowledge one step further after all.

The origin of things in general,

And in particular of fleas, remains

Obscure as ever, spite of all our pains

To trace it : and from egg to flea, from flea

To egg, the interminable pedigree

Would, though less varied, be as vast as those

Which Levy's Duke and Croÿ's Prince suppose

To be their own.   Thy motto, Monarchy,

To fleas doth better than to kings apply.

" *The Flea is dead, long live the Flea!*"   For own,

From dust no royal race was ever known

To spring by mere spontaneous generation,

And even before the King was dead, the Nation

Has sometimes cried " Long live the . . . ! "

" Fabulist,

You know the penalty if you persist

In speaking out of order, so refrain ! "

F

Allow me, Mr. Speaker, to explain
That these irregularities and slips
Are owing to the way in which by skips
And hops the subject moves.　There's no offence !
I scratch my last word out and recommence—

III.

His birthplace mean, his birth undated, born
Among the shavings suffer'd to adorn
The workshed by a carpenter erected,
His education had been much neglected.
But with advantages in vain supplied
To Mediocrity it is the pride
Of Genius to dispense.　The carpenter
That own'd this workshed had a son and heir,
Who was himself a sawyer—not of wood
But bones ; could also blister, purge, let blood,
Deliver ladies who are brought to bed,
Vaccinate babies, lint and plaister spread,
Prescribe in Latin, mix a draught or pill,
And, for a fee extremely moderate, kill
As many patients in an honest way
As any Brook Street doctor.

Now one day

This Flea, who was a flea of intellect,

Seeing the surgeon busily dissect

Dead bodies, was forthwith inspired to try

Experiments in physiology

On living ones.   And 'tis indeed the name

Of Dr. Pulex that has prior claim

To that discovery *de motu cordis*

Et sanguinis, who fame-usurping lord is

Our British Harvey.   Tho' the fact's undated,

A flea it was that first investigated

That most unreasonable tendency

In human blood (which is the reason why

A similar phenomenon we find

In all the reasonings of the human mind)

To keep in vicious circles turning round,

And seek an issue where no issue's found.

IV.

'Tis known that all the famed discoveries

By lesser nations filch'd have had their rise

In some great Frenchman's first instinctive guess ;

Steam, Electricity, the Printing Press,

Gunpowder, and the Laws of Gravitation.

Tom Puce (his private name denotes the nation

Whose native genius in his soul was found)

Reach'd not, however, at a single bound

That grand discovery whereof the fame

Unfairly decorates another's name.

With sunken rocks that treacherously split

The fragile barks by Genius launch'd on it

The Sea of Knowledge teems ; and I suspect

Ambition was the sunken rock that wreck'd

Tom Puce in his first cruize.   But you shall judge.

v.

An unfeed visit, which he did not grudge,

The youthful surgeon every Sunday paid

His pretty cousin, who was waiting-maid

To a young Duchess in the neighbouring town.

Thither one morning, to himself unknown,

Tom Puce he carried in his best cravat.

The tie was loose.   In consequence of that

The pretty cousin with a graceful twist

Adjusted it, as she its owner kist.

This trivial fact was destined to produce

A crisis in the fortunes of Tom Puce.
'Twas not at home he pass'd that night.

VI.

                         They say
Knowledge is Power.   But ah, well-a-day,
Frailty, thy name is . . . Knowledge ! Life attests
The Idyll is a Siren that arrests
The Epos in its passage. As of yore
Discoverers like himself had done before,
Tom Puce to that insidious Siren's charm
Succumb'd—but, like Ulysses, took no harm,
Nor was it *he* that was devour'd.

                        He ow'd
To this, his life's first amorous episode,
The finest passage in that work of his
By Harvey filch'd, *de motu sanguinis.*
But soon ambition in his ardent breast
Was fated to replace love's tenderest
Emotions. For the pretty waiting maid
Was summon'd by the Duchess she obey'd
To dress Her Grace for the Court Ball. O chance
To go to Court! To see the Emperor ! Dance

Even with the Empress !　Such a chance in view,
Farewell all vulgar loves !　Lisette adieu !
Between a Duchess and a Chambermaid
The distance is not *always*, be it said,
A gulf impassable.　This Rubicon
Was cross'd without miscarriage—and anon
The lovely Duchess lost a droplet red
Of that pure blood which, ere her birth, was shed
At Ascalon, Nicæa, Antioch
In bucketfuls abundant . . . . to unlock,
Think you, the Painim's unbelieving hand
From its black grip upon the Holy Land ?
No ! but to found the famous pedigree
Whose forty quarterings fed this favour'd Flea.

VII.

Fleas are dependent on their *entourage*.
Our hero's life here turns a nobler page,
Inscribed no longer with the vulgar name
Of plain Tom Puce, who from this hour became
Known by the title he was born to win,
As the Chevalier de Pucelin.

Now was the time to profit, now or never,

De motu cordis of the great.   What clever

Adventurer (and de Pucelin was both)

Would not, with such an opening, have been loth,

When by a Duchess introduced at Court,　　　'

In his advancing fortunes to stop short

Till he had reach'd ambition's highest pitch ?

Lord President of the Imperial Itch

Might he not be ?   And get himself addrest

As Privy Counsellor the priviest ?

About the Imperial Person day and night,

Chief of Court Vermin, and Grand Parasite !

From nothing need a flea's ambition shrink.

Between all parties the connecting link,

If he to power (as every hero does)

Must wade thro' blood, he mingles as he goes

With every class, and in his own contains

The blood of noble and plebeian veins.

Whig, Tory, Protestant, or Catholic,

All's one to him.   He knows the statesman's
　　　trick

Of using, fusing, and confusing all

The various currents which, inimical

Each to the other's drift when let alone,
By him united serve to speed his own.

On principle despising prejudice
Our Flea, who was in nothing over nice,
—(I say "Our Flea," since in a certain sense
This may by all of us, at whose expense
Fleas thrive, be said of every flea that lives.
For fleas are the true representatives,
The sole successful realized ideal,
Of Socialism, and there's nought unreal
In bloodshed and equality—for fleas,
Who naturally benefit by these.)
—Our Flea, then went to Court. And, with address,
When to the embrace of his fair patroness
The fingers of the Imperial Hand were given
De Pucelin pounced upon them.

VIII.

Gracious heaven!
That high-born hand on whose fair finger tips
The Duchess was about, with perfumed lips,
To press what many a proud moustache in vain

Had often pined and pleaded to obtain—
That scepter'd hand that to the world beneath
Waved life and honours or disgrace and death,
That snowy hand of smiling Majesty
That in it lightly held the mute reply
To Hamlet's monologue—was now, alack,
With a swift gesture of disgust drawn back,
And . . . Ah poor Duchess!

                    Never from that fall
Did she recover.   'Twas observed by all.
Publicity augmented her disgrace,
Though none the private cause of it could trace
In spite of explanations not a few ;
Which only proved, what everybody knew
Or might have known before, that with impunity
No woman can eclipse the fair community
Of her own sex.

IX.

            The Duchess was undone.
And, if the scandal had no further gone
'Twas bad enough.   But libertines begin
Where liberties should end.   De Pucelin,

Hadst thou confined thy galantries audacious
Unto the *baise-main* only . . . but good gracious !
The Lauzuns and the Grammonts of gone days
Whose memoirs scandalize us and amaze
Were not more enterprising.

X.

For a time
Still further on his path of prosperous crime
The gay Chevalier was allowed to get
Unpunish'd, thanks to Courtly Etiquette.
But once the Imperial pageant at an end,
And . . . . Monaldeschi !
Our adventurous friend
Had fared no better than the Swedish Beau
Who for Court favours paid at Fontainebleau
More than their value (and thus here alas
Had closed the life of Tom Puce, *alias*
De Pucelin, *alias* Dr. Pulex, first
Discoverer of the truth, since so disperst,
De motu cordis), if a silken-ear'd
King Charles had not then luckily appear'd
In the Imperial Boudoir.   Entry-free

Are favourite spaniels (lucky dogs they be!)
To approach the Imperial Presence day and night.
And who would squander time, or injure sight,
By looking in a lap-dog's hackled hair
To find one flea?   As soon, by looking there,
You'd find one statesman in St. Stephen's Hall.
There are so many of them, and they all
So hopelessly like one another be!

XI.

The Imperial Spaniel, a Don Juan he,
Had in the Maid of Honour's slim greyhound
His small Zerlina of the moment found.
But his Zerlina's sensitive young heart
Had secretly been wounded with love's dart
By the more massive and majestic grace
Of Beaurevoir, who follow'd to the chase
The Master of the Buckhounds.   Beaurevoir
Had for his humble friend and servitor
Herbault, an honest dog but lowly born,
Who turn'd the kitchen spit from night to morn
The Sire de Pucelin, from dog to bitch
Pursued for ever by the noble itch

For knowledge, whilst neglecting not athletics
Completed thus his course of Cynagetics :
Which brought him by a brief career at last
From Court to Courtyard.   While her husband
    pass'd
His time in turning the Imperial Spit,
Dame Herbault, who was lively, had the wit
To enjoy more tender tasks.   And, thanks to her,
His fortune found occasion to transfer
The Ex-Chevalier de Pucelin
From Madame Herbault on to Haptopin
The butcher's bull-dog.   He migrated then
From Haptopin to Rattler, and again
From Rattler pass'd to Carlin, and at last
From Carlin, back with little Azor, pass'd
To the mean shed where first he came to life.
For Azor's mistress was the lawful wife
Of that shed's lowly lord, the carpenter.

XII.

Thus love's Emotion and Ambition's stir,
  Hair's-breadth Adventures, Contact with the Court,
Science, Romance, and Politics,—in short

The whole career which this discoverer ran
Was doom'd to finish just where it began.
A vicious circle, take it how you will !
But still a circle. And a circle still,
Whether we please to praise it or decry,
Remains the emblem of Eternity.

THE LAST SCENE OF THE PLAY.

BY MRS. W. K. CLIFFORD.

I.

THE village stood half-way up the slope. Behind it rose the mountains. Round it stretched the brown earth almost destitute of trees, of greenness of any sort, but covered by even rows of little dark stumps. They were not more than a foot high, those curious stumps, they looked like little old men, cross and wrinkled. It was difficult to believe that they had ever borne anything good to see or to use. Yet a few months later they would have sent forth long green twigs covered with leaves and heavy with fruit. Of all things seen for the first time, a French or Swiss vineyard is one of the most disappointing ; even at its best, which is not till the summer is waning, its monotony and stuntedness make it utterly unlike the vineyard of imagination. In winter it is barren-looking, dead, and positively ugly.

In front of the village the slopes, crossed and re-crossed by low grey walls dividing off the vineyards, stretched downwards to the white carriage road, to the railway line, to some leafless fruit trees, to some green patches of vegetable garden, to a walk planted on either side with plane trees that, thick and short, interlaced to make a deep shade in summer, but now as bare as the vines, to the blue waters of Lake Leman. Over the lake, and over most things, the sun was shining. It touched the misty clefts in the mountains till each one became a heavenly mystery behind which lay an enchanted land. The Dent du Midi was covered with snow, but the wide dark streaks showed that the sun's power was returning. The mountains that from a distance seemed to form a locked gate to the Rhone valley, as well as the mountains of Savoy, gathered high and close all along the southern side of the lake, even the hills round Glion and Chillon were still white and thick with snow above the line of frequented pathway. But lower down the snow had melted as though the shivering slopes had warmed and comforted themselves against the homes of men. The sun was hot enough for June, but in the shade the cold air and biting wind betrayed their March parentage. Yet there were signs that spring, was already on its way. The few trees huddled round the village, as though they feared the gaunt wastes beyond, were budding. In the markets at Lausanne and Vevey the seed-sellers drove a brisk trade. The little heaps of manure put ready in the vineyards showed that it was nearly time to look after the stumps that as yet were all that represented the coming vintage.

The village consisted of two or three clusters of houses, none of them alike, and none too grand for the thrifty or working-class. A few were picturesque, but the majority were ugly, white-washed, and poor-looking. Here and there the ugliness was relieved by a carved wooden balcony, or an outside staircase, from which hung bunches of yellow corn or pots of greenery fastened up by strings; but the Swiss villager is not over-burdened with a sense of beauty, nor given to spending his time on the decoration of his home.

Standing a little apart from the houses, like a

reverend elder, was an old church with a square tower and faded clock. At the end of the one dead-alive street stood the pump and the inevitable washing-troughs, round which the gossips gathered to idle and the housewives to wash their clothes. A few cobbled-stoned narrow ways, with old high houses warning off the sunshine, wound out of the street or from round odd corners. That was all, save a couple of dreary cafés, and a letter-box, the latter let into a blank wall on which were pasted one or two official notices of the Commune and a placard concerning an Easter concert at Vevey. Few enough were the signs of life, except by the pump, and at stated hours that necessitated going to and fro to transact the trivial business of the day. The children going and coming from school, the cows being taken in and out of the sheds at milking-time, the gathering of letters from the letter-box, the dragging of a load of wood that had come from some mysterious place far out of sight, where trees were plentiful enough to be cut down and sent to villages beyond, a scanty straggling group going towards the cafés

G

after the dinner hour, to which the whole place
held itself sacred ; these were the chief signs of
animation, and for months the only ones. Here
and there, outside the village, was to be seen
a stray house, surrounded by a patch of almost
uncultivated garden, weather-beaten and deserted,
with its shutters closed like the lids of tired eyes.
It was as if, in the drowsy noon or the still cold
night, first one dwelling and then another had
wandered away from the village, and for ever
stayed to dream.   When the spring came they
would all awake, the shutters would be flung
open wide ; the villagers would rouse themselves
and make ready for the summer.   But as yet
there was only the sunshine, just a hint that
Heaven was not forgetful ; that the world would
soon be beautiful once more, and its people must
awake to behold it.

Far up behind the village, so far that it was beyond
the vineyards and the little meadows that were growing
green again, just at the edge of the fir-trees that clothed
the topmost part of the mountain, stood a long low
building ; its whiteness could be seen for miles

away. Close beside it was a ruined wooden châlet
with piles of grey stones near it. Yet, though hands
had surely placed the stones in heaps quite lately,
there was not a sign of life anywhere about; nothing
but the firs above, and the slope beneath with the
village half-way down towards the lake. Midway
between the firs and the village stood the highest inhabited house in the immediate vicinity—one of those
houses that seemed to have strayed from its fellows
and stood conspicuously apart.

The house was only one story high, with a window
at the back looking up at the firs and the ruined châlet
and shed, and a door and several windows on the other
side looking down towards the village and the lake.
Before the upper windows stretched a wooden balcony
and from it hung great bunches of maize corn. Round
the house was a patch of garden-ground that had lately
been dug over, and here and there displayed a few
homely vegetables doing fairly well in the keen March
winds. The garden and the maize corn were the only
signs of eating and drinking and waking humanity.
The door was shut, the windows closed, the green
shutters fastened inside so that no gust disturbed

G 2

them ; there was no smoke from the chimney; the
house seemed simply a part of the landscape and the
stillness.

But above the stillness was broken. In the ruined
châlet there was a sound of some one moving
cautiously. Between the wide chinks a man's eyes
looked out as far as they could see, again and
again down at the slope, at the lonely house, and
anxiously towards the village. At last, seemingly
satisfied that no one was watching him, he
came cautiously out from his shelter, and, keeping
close to the low grey wall, began to descend. He
almost bent double as he advanced as if to avoid
being seen ; he hurried and yet took each step
with care, casting a glance about him every
moment. He drew near the house with a sigh of
relief, keeping in a line with it as soon as its
height formed a screen between him and the
village. He stole to the front door with noiseless
steps, and, lifting the latch, entered. There was a
long dim passage, bare and white-washed, flagged
with rough grey stones. At the farther end was a
wooden staircase ; he looked towards it anxiously

and listened. To his left there was suddenly the sound of a wheezing cough. He heard it with an air of relief. He turned and examined the fastenings of the street-door; they consisted of a lock and a bolt; he drew the bolt, and turning the key in the lock, took it out. Then opening a door on the left he entered a dirty comfortless kitchen. At a glance he noticed that the windows were fastened inside the closed shutters. An old woman rose as he entered. He gave her the key of the door.

"Some one might come for us," he said. "Do not let in any visitors to-day, we have letters to write and wish to be quiet, and if anyone comes to see you there is no need to say that the artist has gone and we are here. I have locked the door and taken out the key, so that if any people come they may think the house is empty. Let them knock." She looked at him suspiciously. "It is only for to-day," he added. "To-morrow it will be different."

"I will not say that Monsieur the painter is gone," she answered. "I will not let in anyone unless the knocking is so loud I cannot help it."

He nodded, and left her looking at the key. The English were strange people, she thought, it was of no use suspecting them, for there was no knowing what even the best of them would do; and she sat down to consider. The painter who had stayed in her house since January painting the snow-covered mountains had been gone a fortnight. The day before he went he had talked with a stranger who had looked over his canvass while he sat painting near Vevey. He had always loved to talk, had the painter. A foolish waste of time it seemed to the old woman, who had lived long years almost in silence. For work and talk were never trusty partners; if one was good for aught the other went for little. But the painter had told the stranger how he had lived for two months in her house, pointing it out on the slope, and that the next day he was going to Italy. He went, and that same night the strangers came. They told her not to say that the painter had gone and they had come, for they wanted to be alone and quiet. The lady was ill and suffering. The old woman was to forget if she could that she had changed her tenant. They asked the painter's name,

then said theirs was the same, and they expected no
letters, no friends ; they wanted to be alone and quiet.
Well, they were curious people, were the English,
always liking to keep to themselves. These were easy to
do for, quiet enough, staying up in their rooms almost
in silence. She would have forgotten that they were
there but for the serving of meals. She doubted
if the village knew that they were there, for the
painter had walked away in the early morning with
all he possessed on his back, and the same evening these two had walked in with all they possessed
in their hands, and neither had passed through
the village. It was just as well ; Louis Strubb would
not come asking for his money. The painter was
known to be poor, for how could a man who sat
all day before an easel be rich ? But this Englishman who was able to travel with his wife might well
be supposed to pay more, and Louis Strubb was
not one to wait patiently if he could help it. She
had noticed that each time the Englishman went
out he avoided the village : none could know that he
had come. To-morrow at the market, if any one had
seen him, there might be questions asked, and Louis

Strubb made wiser. But that was in the future. To-day there was nothing to disturb her, nothing to trouble about till it was time to prepare the strangers' supper at seven. No need either to think of that yet, nor to burn the wood in waste. For a while she could rest, forgetting that she was cold. Ah, that was comfortable, a chair and a high stool on which to put her legs; she was tired and nearly sleeping. And why not sleep? Good dreams might come of youth—a foolish time when one loitered and laughed over-much, yet pleasant to dream of when one's limbs ached and there was little to do but rest. Her head fell on her chest, her withered eyes closed, the wrinkles in her face smoothed away, and all things were forgotten for a little space as she sat and dozed beside the cold black stove.

II.

The man went slowly up the creaking stairs which turned abruptly towards the front of the house and faced a door at the top. Between the door and the last stair there was a landing which went along the width of the house; and on to it opened all the

rooms of the top story. He opened the door facing
the stairs ; and entered a bare, silent room, which
the old woman beneath called the *salon.* There was
a second door, leading to an inner room ; he went
towards it and listened, then opened it gently and
looked in. The inner room was furnished as a bedroom, dim, from the closed shutters, and chilly, for
the sunshine passing over the house had left it in
shade. On one of the two low beds a woman was
lying. She was dressed, her head was pillowed high,
and her arms thrown back beneath it raised it still
higher. She was young, but worn and haggard-
looking. She was beautiful, or would have been so
but for a look of anguish that seemed to have become
a settled expression on her face. She started as the
man entered, and in a voice that was full of dread
asked, " Is it all right ? " He nodded. With a sigh of
relief she sank back.

" It is very cold," he said ; " you had better lie
still—do you hear ? " for she had collapsed in some
strange way, and turned her eyes from him. " I will
call you presently ; I want to be alone a little while."
There was a certain power in his voice that seemed to

render the woman helpless. She made a sign of assent, then looked up, and having answered simply " Yes," turned her face away till it was almost hidden in the pillow. He glanced quickly at the door leading to the landing, and saw that it was locked. He went back to the *salon* and closed the bedroom door behind him. For a moment he looked out, through the green bars of the closed shutters, at the village below, at the lake with the sunshine sparkling on it, at the Savoy mountains, with the little towns and villages set low down along the shore. If he were only across that bit of blue water scrambling up the snow-covered heights, or speeding along in the train towards Bellegarde, he might yet escape unnoticed. He turned away and looked round the comfortless room. He had a way of taking in his surroundings quickly and keenly. The room was bare, and, like the rest of the house inside and out, whitewashed. There was a round table, a gaunt sofa, two or three chairs : a wide, open fireplace with a few logs piled up ready for lighting on its stone cheeks. That was all, save that between the windows stood a high, well-made escritoire. It had a flap that let

down in front to form a desk; beneath the flap
there were several drawers, and behind it several
smaller ones. He let down the flap ready to write,
then opened a drawer and took out an old photograph, faded and yellow. It had the indescribable
look of a portrait of some one who was dead.
That old woman with the long, thin face, and
prim cap, could not be living. He looked at it
tenderly, put it on the mantelshelf, then, going back
to the escritoire, sat down to write. It was a little
difficult to see; there was almost a recess between
the windows, and the shadow kept off the light. A
single moment would have sufficed to open the
shutters and make the whole room lovely with the
sunshine without, with the landscape looking in,
but he did not dare to risk it. He put a sheet of
paper, before him, and glanced uneasily about before
beginning. It was a sort of relief to see his
mother's portrait on the shelf. Something unde-
fined seemed to be standing by him, to be watching him, to fill the whole room with a strange
presence. The woman on the low bed in the inner
room felt it too; it filled all the space about them

both. The man defied it, the woman quailed before
it with agonized shrinking. In every atom of the air
there seemed to be a suggestion of consciousness. It
gave the one a vague knowledge of what was coming,
it sent a sick dread into the heart of the other to
share its bitter anguish.

The man began his letter almost desperately,
feeling that he was writing it against time and in
the teeth of many things. The light changed and
fell upon his face. It was thin and weary, but it
had none of the sadness or the fear of the
woman's. He was singularly handsome, tall and
well-made ; perhaps he should be described as dark.
There was something in his eyes difficult to
fathom—a light, a spark almost, an expression
that made the whole face a puzzle. It gave
him at times an uncanny—a shifty—at others a
kindly humorous look. There was a changefulness
about the face that seemed to make the whole
man an uncertainty to everyone in everything, a
man who for some reason almost beyond his control could not be counted on in any way. He
somehow conveyed the impression that he was

capable of doing great deeds and generous ones
if they were suggested to him and came easy, without in the least seeing their greatness or generosity;
or of committing almost any crime, any meanness,
if they too came in his way or were convenient,
never realizing or caring about the enormity or the
meanness.   Good and evil had been settled and defined by others, but he was not able to distinguish
accurately between them, or to care which was which.
In a certain sense he was morally blind as some
are colour-blind.   He did that which came in his
way, which seemed easiest; the goodness or the
badness did not concern him.   People   might
applaud one deed, and be shocked at another.   To
him in a way they were the same.   He was glad
if people liked what he did; if they did not, he
shrugged his shoulders; he could not help it.   The
one real guide he acknowledged was his own feeling, the general convenience of himself and, occasionally, of those immediately about him.   Of
very strong feeling he was almost destitute, of a
queer analytical one he was constantly possessed.
Perhaps it was this that put the uncanny look

into his eyes. They were the eyes of some other person looking on at himself, occasionally those of a mocking fiend who was his master. He was distinctly a man who attracted women. It was impossible to help thinking that many had probably loved him. But men were more cautious. In all his life but one man had been his true and fast friend. How true that one had been he had reason to know well, and yet, unable to put absolute confidence in anybody, he had many a time weighed in a mental balance the one friendship that had never failed him. It was three years since he had dared to see that friend, but he was writing to him now :—

"DEAR JACK,

"To-day I got a paper at Vevey, and see they have tracked us to Lausaune. They will probably not be long in scenting the rest of the trail. To-night we—or I, at any rate—make an effort to get elsewhere. Meanwhile do not be nervous. I shall not be taken alive. After all, Death is but a scene-shifter, but I prefer giving him the signal

myself to leaving it to others. I hope that meddling
fool, her brother, will be content when he finds that
I have escaped him, as I shall do anyway, dead or
alive, and that he will not give you any trouble.
But I know nothing of legal matters, and, as you
see, mean to keep clear of them.

> " Yours, old fellow,
>
> " H. W."

He went to the window again and carefully
scrutinized the landscape ; then to the back of the
house, and looked up at the ruined châlet, the
dark firs, the upper paths that led to higher
villages out of sight. He shook his head and
returned to the *salon.* " I suppose it is always
so ; every place seems safe till one gets to it, and
then every other seems safer. I must try Charlotte
soon." He went to the escritoire and half-hesi-
tatingly opened the deepest drawer inside the flap.
He drew out a small pair of Derringers. They
were loaded. With grim satisfaction he examined
and replaced them. For a moment he stood uncertain, facing the room, as if almost he were trying

to understand some hidden thing, to force his
perceptions into the future, to get some help, some
direction for the present. Then, as if he recognized
the folly of inactivity, or hesitation, he went forward
quickly and called the woman from the inner room.

"Charlotte!"—he opened the door and looked
in. She started to her feet, almost as if she were
scared.

"Yes—is it anything?"

"Well—no," he answered in a leisurely voice, in
which there was no alarm though a suggestion of doubt-
fulness. "But I think it would be as well to have a
talk. We are pretty silent as a rule." She came
slowly into the *salon*, a tall, slight woman with a pale
face, and eyes that were full of fear and sorrow. Her
mouth was curved and beautifully formed, her hair
was dark, and gathered back into a knot behind.
She looked like a loving, tender, woman, yet there
was an air of strength and determination about her,
a manner that made her seem reserved and cold.
She had probably been counted both in the days of
her happiness and beauty. She hesitated at the
doorway ; the grey light, her own pale face and plain

black dress, all made her look taller than she actually was. She seemed to sway to and fro for an instant, almost as if she were tottering. She went to the window and looked out, but the brightness blinded, almost frightened her, and with a shudder she turned away and stood leaning against the escritoire, waiting for her husband to speak. He scanned her face in an odd, reflective manner.

"It is strange that you should feel it so much more than I," he said.

"Do you not feel it?" she asked passionately, clasping her hands. She had a deep sweet voice; it was the voice of a woman who could suffer sorely and love well. A voice to which it was impossible to help listening, one realized so keenly the living woman behind it.

" I suppose I do as much as anyone can ; but men take things calmly. Besides when a deed is done no amount of feeling will undo it."

" Harford," she cried, yet she spoke in so low a tone that the keenest ears beyond the room could not have caught a sound, "is it true? That is what I am always asking myself—is it a dream, or madness,

H

or truth? It has come on me so suddenly I cannot take it in. I feel as if you cannot have lived these two years since we have been married, these three since she died,—you could not have lived so calmly through them if it were true." He looked at her, the strange expression was in his eyes, he seemed to be watching the effect of every word he said.

"It is true," he answered doggedly, "as true as it is that you stand there. I gave her enough poison to kill half a dozen women. If any doctor but Jack had been called in, there would have been but one thing for him to do——." She writhed in agony at every word he said, shrinking involuntarily farther away from him. He saw it plainly enough, but it produced no visible effect upon him, except that the odd interested look on his face grew more intense, as though he were making an experiment and keenly watching the effect. She raised her head for a moment, he saw that her lips were white, he looked gravely into her eyes.

"How could you live?" she cried. "The shame, the horror, the remorse, why did they not kill you? They seem to be killing me now. In every sound there is a taunt, a threat, a reproach, and everywhere I see a dead woman's face—the face of the woman you killed—I can see her even at this moment as plainly as though she were between us,—her closed eyes and still lips and folded hands. O God, Harford, how could you?" but her words had no effect on him.

"It is very odd," he repeated, "but it seems as if it had cost you, these last few days since you knew, as much as it has cost me all these years since it was done." She did not answer, she felt bitterly that it was true. The crime had been his; the agony and remorse, the horror and the dread were hers, and she had borne it all in the last few days in which she had known.

"Has it cost you nothing?" she asked.

"I think it has," he said, "it has not left me many minutes' peace since it was done. Only men don't take their pain in the concentrated manner of women."

There was a ring of truthfulness in his voice that was some sort of relief to her. She felt as if she could bear anything better than the terrible callousness that

H 2

had added a sting, if a sting were possible, to the knowledge that had come upon her.

¯ "Why has it been so suddenly discovered now, and why—why did you do it—how could you?" She burst out speaking of the thing directly for the first time.

"I bore it as long as I could, but she made life such that it came to be impossible for us both to live in the same world.   It was after our long quarrel, after I heard that you had come back, and gradually I got possessed of the idea that she or I must die. She felt ill, and the devil suggested how it could be managed. I got Jack to come and see her. He being a doctor I thought it would make things right, and that it would never occur to him to suspect.   But it did. He discovered it the moment he saw her, but she was then past saving. He would have had me hanged if I had not prevailed on him at last to hold his tongue. "They'll make him pay for that now, I fear," he added, uneasily.   "He agreed to be silent for the sake of bygones and for my mother's sake," (and he looked towards the faded photograph); "it was when she was failing, and he knew that betraying me would be killing her. Perhaps he thought it was enough to kill one woman between us." He was silent a moment as if he expected her to speak, but she did not make a sign. "He made me promise not to marry you," he went on, "but I broke that promise ; it was not in human nature to keep it. I had married the other woman only in a fit of jealousy, it was not possible to miss the chance when it came, and I found you cared for me still." But the last words only made her draw back a little farther from him, and she was silent.

"Did she love you ? " she asked at last almost in a whisper. He was silent for a moment ; he seemed to call up some past scene in his mind, before he answered :

"Well, yes," he said slowly, "she did. I wish she hadn't ; it was long enough before I could get rid of the memory of her eyes following me round and round that room, and looking up gratefully when I gave her the dose that finally killed her." She locked her teeth to keep her lips still. She could see it all as clearly as if now the woman lay dying once more before him. But his voice was just the same.

She wrenched her thoughts from the dead woman to the living man.

"Why did no one suspect before?"

"It was no one's business to do so. There was a chattering servant ready to say what she only half thought, but when no fuss was made, and the doctor asked no questions, she forgot it. I gave her ten pounds when she went away, and perhaps she understood she was to hold her tongue. It would never have come out if Tom Carr had not come back; he always hated me, and he was always suspicious. He went poking about, and got hold of a chemist's assistant and of Jack, though Jack said nothing; but that only made matters worse. Then it occurred to the meddling fool to get an order to have the body exhumed. He managed it somehow; I heard it from Jack. He had never spoken to me since the hour we parted by her coffin. But he gave me the hint and we fled. It was lucky we had arranged to go to Italy that very day. No one suspected it was flight, and we got a start."

"And if they find you?" she whispered.

"If they take me, the rest will be easy—for them," he said quietly.

" Are you certain they can prove it ? "

He smiled grimly.

" I was a novice in the art, and merely put the proof into a cupboard till it should occur to someone to look for it. It has been looked for and found; it is virtually proved against me as clearly as if I had given her the dose in public. One would have thought the grave was a good hiding-place, but it has been a bad one." She hardly heard the last words. The crime and his calm relation of it were so awful, and, besides that, there was the dread of what might overtake him.

" If they should find you ? " she gasped.

" If they took me there would be—the hangman's rope," he said quietly. She raised her hand quickly to her lips to stop a cry that rose to them. Even then he watched her cruelly. "It would not hurt much, it would soon be over. There may be something to come." He said the last words as if he were doubtful, yet politely curious concerning eternity. " I have drained life pretty dry," he added. She remembered an account of an

execution she had once read. Something had seemed
to force her to read it, but for days afterwards it had
haunted her. The prisoner was taken from his cell
— she dimly saw the ghastly procession that was
formed — the death-bell tolling, the parson in his
surplice reading the Burial Service over the living
man—into a stone yard it went, and the hangman
was there, he stood beside the man—O God, had
she been there ! She could see and hear it all. Was
it coming true—true of Harford !

"Would there be no escape ?" she asked in an
agonized voice she could not raise above a whisper.
"Surely it would be better to die first—anything
rather than that." He was silent for a moment.
A gleam of triumph came into his eyes. He opened
the deep drawer behind the flap.

"Yes," he said, almost with a smile, and pointed
to the drawer. She turned slowly and looked in,
then raised her eyes enquiringly to his. In some
strange way he seemed to know how it would all
be. He took up one of the Derringers and put it
to his head, "it will be time enough when they
are three steps from the door," he said. A little

sense of relief went through her. He had, at any rate, courage for that. She lifted his right hand, but dropped it quickly with a shudder, and, taking up the left one, kissed it—a hurried, frightened kiss. For one short moment her eyes reflected the triumph of his.

"One is enough to kill?" she asked.

"One is enough," he answered.

"The other will do for me."

He looked at her silently; he knew well enough that she meant it. "For you?"

"Yes, for me," she said, firmly.

"I don't think you would take life easily without me," he said, slowly.

Her lips gave but one word—"No."

He considered for a moment. "I don't see why we should not go on together if we are forced to use them," and he touched the drawer. "I believe," he added, and there was an odd sound in his voice, "I believe every atom of me would know it if your lips ever touched another man's, though I were dust being swept before a March wind like that that howled round us last night."

She did not answer, the words seemed so out of place, so foreign to all things possible : they fell almost unnoticed on the space about them. For a few moments there was silence again. The cold inside the room had become intense; its emptiness exaggerated, as though something had previously been in it; the strange atmosphere that had hung over it, had somehow vanished, had gone seeking, perhaps, the fate that was nearing the two who stood together. Outside the sun was still shining, the lake sparkling, the little villages across it standing out distinctly in the clear afternoon light. He saw them through the bars of the shutters, and she, following the direction of his eyes, understood his thoughts. The room was like a prison, yet it felt insecure, as though already it were known and watched. Her teeth chattered with cold, her limbs trembled, her icy hands went for a moment round her throat seeking the little warmth gathered at the back beneath the coil of hair resting low in the nape of her neck. Suddenly she looked up at the man beside her, at his tall figure, at his handsomeness, at his strange, uncertain eyes. She had been very

happy with him, and proud of him. There had
been phases during their married life when he
had been cold and strange, but never a time,
never since she had first known him, when she had
not loved him, when he had not seemed like
no other man on earth. It was all over. For
ever and for ever finished. There was nothing in
the living world that could adjust things, no chances,
no possibilities that could set them right; nothing
that could bring to life a dead woman—a woman
whose white face and closed eyes were always before
her as though in some dim shadow. They waited,
she did not dare to think for what? She stood
staring at the terrible realities, quaking miserably
alike at the past and at the future that was swiftly
coming; she could almost see it now before her.
He, watching her, understood something of what
was in her heart. A sense of shame stole
over him, and of utter helplessness. He felt
that she had been looking back into the memories
of years, that in a measure she had softened towards
him. He knew perfectly all that he had been to
her. He put out his hand to touch hers. She drew
back, but more gently than before.

"Wont you kiss me," he said. "It will probably be all over soon. Wont you kiss me, Charlotte? My wife, wont you kiss me once more?"

His words were almost passionate, but his voice was still only curious, his eyes were shifting, he was still in a measure experimenting upon her. He had loved her in the past, and he remembered it; but it was doubtful if he actually loved her much now. She had become so truly a part of his life that he could not separate it from his own, nor endure the thought of separation, and for that same reason he was cruel and merciless to her as to himself; curious for her fate as for his own, and, so long as it did not sever itself from his, almost careless of what she suffered. She heard his words, but did not move till he repeated them. Then she dragged herself a step towards him and with an effort put up her face. The touch of his went through her. With a shudder she put the knowledge of all things from her. Her whole heart filled with tenderness—miserable aching tenderness. Weary and desperate she felt as if for a single moment she must feel herself clasped to him once more, it might be for the last time on earth.

He bent down to put his face against hers ; and so there came to him a moment's rest and satisfaction— the only living rest that was possible to him in all the world.

"God help me, Charlotte," he said. "Let me be what I may, I have loved you with all my heart." The shifty look had gone from his eyes, his voice was natural. It was as if his life, touching hers, was for a moment purified in it ; as if the evil that had possessed him stood a little way off, waiting till she had drawn apart from him. "But you shudder when you come near me now, you are afraid—— "

"No, no," she said, "not of you; but it seems sometimes as if a mocking fiend possessed you. It is not you of whom I am afraid, but of that—and of what you did."

"Have you any love for me still ? " he asked half desperately, half curiously. She did not answer for a moment. He looked down at her face and mentally traced out the lines that misery had drawn on it. "I can feel that it is all gone," he said cynically, watching her closely, "you only loved the good in me, and there was never much of that,

You only loved me while it was easy and convenient. Now you are only doing your duty, trying to bear with me. Women are much alike." He seemed to be comparing her to someone unseen. She looked at him almost in wonder, she raised herself from his arms and spoke in a low voice that seemed to come from the depth of her soul.

"There has never been a time when I have not loved you," she said, "not since the day we met first when I was a little girl still, and we sat on the grass and picked daisies while our fathers talked. It has grown with me and strengthened with me ; it is my life to love you, a thing I cannot shake off. Even though it shrinks from you or makes no sign, it is there—but this " she said clasping her hands " kills me. It is worse than death. I know I shrink from you and shudder, and dread your touch and shiver at your voice, at your step, and yet I love you. O God, if I could give my body and soul for ever and ever to be burnt for you so that you might be pure again, so that you might be without that crime upon you, it would be sweeter than heaven, far." For a moment she stopped. He did not speak. It was so strange to him this intense love—a love of which he himself had never been capable, though he had loved the woman before him better than any other. He looked on as a spectator at that which was written in her eyes, almost afraid of it, though fear of anything else in the world he had none. It was a thing beyond his ken, beyond his grasp, a strange odd thing of which he had been well enough aware before, yet had never wholly realized. He stood waiting for her to speak again, in doubt, almost in awe, like one who has strayed into a church and stands before the altar of a religion at which he has sometimes scoffed but suddenly feels to be true. "It is my life, my unutterable woe to love you," she went on, "do not doubt me or think that I shall fail you because I cannot kiss you or let your arms go round me now. There is something stronger in me than my shrinking self, something that clings to you, though I stand here, and that cannot swerve from you."

"Not though you know me now for a coward and a murderer?" he asked.

The bitter tears fell down her face, the cold

unconscious tears of woe, too great to find other expression.

"No," she said slowly, "not even though I know you are a murd"——but her lips refused to say the word. "Oh that I could have been both for you," she cried passionately, bowing her head, " could have done the crime and borne the load, and you never knowing." She put her face down in her hands and rested them on the escritoire. But still he stood silent, almost ashamed, seeing all things clearly as though a door had opened, gazing in speechless wonder at the woman who was his wife.

"I cannot tell," he said at last, "what put it into your head to care for me. I have never been fit for you for one single moment in my whole life."

"Oh, yes, yes, you have been, but for this terrible crime."

" No. I was never worth your loving," he said in a low voice, "and yet though I have been not only what you know now, but everything else on earth that was bad, I have loved you." As if her measure were not quite full, some fiend put a sudden thought into her heart. She raised her head and looked at him eagerly.

" Harford," she said, in a voice that had changed altogether, " You have loved me—well and truly? Tell me that, let me know that, though I do know it, but let me hear you say it." There was no doubt of this in her heart, it was but to hear him say it, to have his own testimony to his own truth of which she was certain. But he turned his eyes from hers; he could not meet them, and was silent. A new terror possessed her, a strange numbness stole over her. " I do not mean that time before, but since we were married, dear," she said entreatingly, and a world of tenderness came into her voice. " Since I have been your wife you have loved me truly and been faithful?" But still he did not move. There was a long moment's silence before he spoke.

" There shall be no lie between us now, Charlotte," he said, and turned to look at her, but he could not meet her eyes. " I have not even been faithful to you. Yet I have loved you, do not doubt that. You have been the one woman in the world to me."

" And yet not faithful even to her?" she said, look-

I

ing up with eyes that wondered what demon it was
that had put her heart beneath his feet. She could
not say another word, her life seemed to wane, her
heart almost to lose its sense of suffering, her senses
to stupefy. The whole world had betrayed her, a
great avalanche had overwhelmed her. She looked
at the sofa, and with her eyes measured the distance
between it and the escritoire; with uncertain steps she
reached it and hid her face on the hard square
pillow. There are limits even to human capacity to
feel pain. She sat still and almost senseless, the sight
of everything hidden from her, yet understanding
plainly all that had overtaken her; as though unable
to bear the load longer, she had put it down before
her to contemplate.

The man looked at her wonderingly, doubtful what
to do, cursing the folly that had made him betray
himself. He had had other things to say when he
called her from the inner room. There was a matter
of life and death to arrange, and arrange quickly, and
as yet he had not even entered upon it. For a few
moments he stood considering, then, kneeling by the
sofa, he leant over her.

"Charlotte," he said tenderly, "look up. You were always the bravest woman on earth. You are not going to break down now?"

"No," she said bitterly, "you need not fear that."

"You women cannot understand men, the power that mere flesh and blood has over them, and yet the little difference it makes to their best feelings. I have never swerved from you in my heart, even when I have been falsest to you. I have loved no other woman on earth, could have endured life with no other, have trusted thoroughly no other human being. Men and women are so different; a man can separate life, feeling one thing for one woman and one thing for another, yet truly love just one. A woman puts all she has on one man, and would think anything short of that treason. I have been a base wretch, a scoundrel, everything that is bad, but you have been the one woman of my life; any good that was in me, any strength, has been spent in loving you, only the badness and weakness have gone elsewhere." She raised her head. Her face was proud and white. She looked like a statue come to life to know life's keenest misery.

I 2

"I only saw the good, I did not think the other existed. It seems as if there had been two men, one my husband, the other some fiend that mocked and tempted him and used him as its puppet."

"That is so, Charlotte," he answered simply. She lifted her eyes to his face—the dear face she had loved so well. Good or bad, he was everything to her even now—just her own life, and she clung to him as the shipwrecked soul clings with despairing hands to the battered, broken thing that was once a ship with a freight of happy life; clings desperately, knowing that when it is gone there will be only the black water and the everlasting silence.

"If we could get away into some other world together——" she began with lips that quivered.

"We will, we must," he said bitterly.

"Leaving all things behind, all that has brought us this woe and misery, and begin some new life together—if we could die out of this one we have known, and begin all things afresh," she went on with a voice full of infinite longing after all that she knew and felt was for ever at an end.

"My dear," he said gently, "we must. In one form or other we must simply die, either by those," and made a sign towards the drawer with the pistols, "or living, we must vanish and leave no track behind."

"Why?" She put aside the pain that was eating into her heart, to gather strength to face what was coming. "Why," she repeated, for he half hesitated, as if he were loth to break in upon her momentary calmness, her ghost of a dream of a future.

"I think we are getting towards the end," he said slowly, "that this is somehow," and he looked round the cold bare room, "the last scene of the play."

"What do you mean—tell me." She put her hands on his shoulders and forgot everything but his danger.

"I called you just now to break it to you——"

"Have they traced us?"

"Pretty nearly," he said, and the old calm manner came back as he found himself on the ordinary lines of practical life again. "This morning I bought a paper at Vevey. They have traced us to Lausanne, they will not be long doing the rest. I came back by the upper paths again and looked round the fir-wood above, there is no practicable escape in that direction. But we must get from here at once—as soon as it is dark to-night."

"Why not now?"

"We may be watched, we should certainly be seen. I have planned it all. They may be a little time getting the clue to us; they may not know in the village that the artist has gone and we are here, no one saw us come or has seen us since. To-night, when the old woman is asleep, I will make a new start——"

"You?" He felt the tug had come. He knew she would help him, but whether she would trust him too he was curious to find out. For he did not know himself what the result of his going would be, even though he escaped safely. How much he still cared for her and how necessary he would find her he wanted to prove. He had not been able to help wondering how it would feel to be cut adrift, absolutely adrift, from all his present ties and surroundings. The sensations of beginning life again a free man, he felt, would be so exciting.

The thought of them made him eager. He was always anxious to see the next moment, to know what might be its secret. He had this feeling, and this only, regarding even death. In death there would be certain escape from the present, and possibly life—life of a sort beyond human experience. He was in no hurry, he was willing to go on here if it could be managed. After all, this world might contain many surprises yet; but if it refused him liberty, or threatened still worse, there was the Derringer. In a moment he could give life the slip, and perhaps from across the strange boundary look back, unseen and triumphant, at the things that had perplexed him, the things that in the end he had baffled. Meanwhile he looked curiously at the woman before him, weighing the probabilities that suggested themselves.

"You?" she repeated. She seemed to know what he was going to propose, to divine what was in his thoughts.

"I think it would be better for me to go alone, if you have nerve to stay; I have thought it all out. I can disguise myself a little and get over the hills behind to the Rhone valley. Perhaps I could cross the lake unnoticed by one of the morning steamers, from a station further on towards Chillon ; this end may be watched. So I may get over to Savoy, and there trust to chance, or I may push along the valley and over some lonely pass into Italy."

"And I ? "

"And you must stay and pretend that I am ill to the woman below. She need not enter the bed-room, and will think I am there. I must devise some means of letting you know where I am. I will think it over before I start. There will be money at Vevey. You must manage to get it and, when it is safe, to come to me. I cannot live long without you, but they know we are together and are less likely to trace us if I start alone. Besides you could not walk and bear the fatigue that I can. You see I have thought it out. Can you do it ? "

"Yes, I can do it," she answered gently. "You know that. You had better go as soon as it is dark. You will get farther on by the morning, and may even get an early train unsuspected." She had seen it all in her mind. "It must be getting late, the sun has

been behind the house this long time. You must
have food. At seven the woman will bring our supper;
she had better see you——." She stopped, he was
not attending to her words but to something farther
off, to something outside.

"I thought I heard a footstep go round the
house," he said. They stood up and listened, for a
moment she felt paralysed. He opened the door, and
looked down the stairs, all was dusky and silent.
The woman beneath was still sleeping beside the
empty stove. He went along the landing to the
window at the back of the house and peered out.
He came back quickly, his face pale and determined.
He hurried towards the closed shutters and looked
through the bars. Then he turned quietly round.

"It is too late," he said, "we are surrounded back
and front. They are at the door." For a moment
she stood helplessly looking at him, then the dazed
feeling seemed to pass from her.

"What must we do?" she asked, in the voice of a
woman awaking.

"There is only one thing; there is no other
chance left." His anxiety to see how she would act

now that the crisis that would test her had come seemed to be his strongest feeling.

"Is there no escape?" she gasped.

"None. We will be absolutely certain first; but half-a-dozen men can hardly be round the house for any other purpose." They stood by the open door of the *salon*, he with his arm just touching her waist, yet drawing back a little, she leaning forward, her face ashy white, her eyes flashing with a strange fire.

There was a loud knock at the barred front door; with a wild throb her heart echoed it. They could almost hear the old woman start from her sleep. She pushed back the stool on which her legs had rested; it made a loud grating noise on the stone floor. The knocking was repeated. The two listening above drew closer together. The man cast a hurried glance at the escritoire behind, calculating in his mind the number of seconds it would take to reach it. They heard the old woman go slowly towards the door. The man looked at his wife. The moment had come. He made a step towards the escritoire. With a cry she threw her arms round him, kissing his eyes, and mouth, and neck as if with those last kisses she would draw her whole soul into her heart.

"I will not live one hour without you, my love, my life. Oh, if I could but give you my life, my soul, and take yours into mine!"

"You forgive me?" he said grimly, smoothing back her hair, and looking at her face as he held it between his two hands. The strange light was in his eyes; even in that last moment he could not give himself up wholly to a passionate farewell. He was alive to the finger-tips with the whole situation, curiously waiting to see what the next thing would be in this world or the other. Her agony was odd to him even then, but a great tenderness came into his heart, a great gratitude to this pure woman who had loved him. He could see their two lives before him, their two souls, hers in its whiteness and agony clinging to him hopelessly. For the first time he shuddered, though only for a moment, at his own past. He kissed her, and in that last kiss there came the strange feeling that it was sacrilege in him to touch her. There seemed to sweep over him the sudden knowledge that here they parted. Here life ended,

and, in any life to come, together they would be no
more. Already space seemed to be wrenching them
apart. Clearly before his eyes he saw the loneliness
of eternity, an eternity in which never more would
they be together. His heart grew cold, and
it seemed as if he saw and understood all things
in the hour that was for ever too late. But he made
no sign. "You forgive, my darling, I know
that," he said with a long sigh, and then his
composure and coolness came back to serve him
to the end.

"Forgive you?" she cried, with a long, yearning
look up into his face. "Don't ask me *that*. You
know. You are my life, my heaven, my eternity—
there is none other for me, and I will have none
other. Do life and heaven ask forgiveness?" The
door had been opened below, as in a dream they had
heard their own names uttered. There were voices
and steps coming along the passage, already at the
foot of the stairs. There was not a moment left;
he looked at her. She understood. Her head had
been on his breast—she lifted it; her tender hands
let go—and they had parted. He took the pistols

from the drawer; he hid one under the hard cushion of the sofa, looking at her meaningly with the gleam of triumph in his eyes. The footsteps came round the bend in the creaking stairs. She nodded to him, with a scared look on her face, but he was satisfied. He knew she would not fail. The men coming up were in sight of the doorway. In a second she was outside it, holding the door-handle behind in her hands. Tall and erect she stood, without a sign of fear, and faced them.

"What do you want?" she asked. For a moment they hesitated, as if uncertain what to do. Her hands trembled, otherwise she did not stir, but like a flash it went through her that she was holding the door to while her husband died.

"Mrs. Harford Wilson?" one of the strange men said in English.

"Yes, Mrs. Harford Wilson," she answered defiantly. Her heart throbbed. What did it mean, the strange silence behind. Had he faltered? Was he to be taken after all—taken and hanged as a felon. She could see the executioner beside him. Could he have found some strange means of escape? She had left him with the pistol in his hand. She remembered the second one ready beneath the sofa-cushion.

" Madame," said an old man with a silver-headed stick (he was the representative of the police from the village), " you must stand aside, we have to arrest your husband." They advanced a step. They were four stairs from the top, within two yards of her. She grasped the handle more tightly, almost supporting herself by it, but her calmness staggered the men before her. She looked scornfully at the old man who had spoken.

" We have a warrant for his apprehension on the charge of murder," the Englishman said in the business voice of an officer of the law. " You must stand aside," and he advanced, " or we shall be obliged to use force and "———there was a sharp report, the sound of a heavy fall. The men started back for a second in dismay. The woman's hands fell from the door-handle and with a click the door opened for an inch or two. A shock seemed to go through her, yet for a second there was a smile of triumph on her lips, the gleam that had been in the man's eyes seemed to pass through hers, then a cry burst from her.

"You can enter, there is only a dead man there," she said, and fell senseless across the doorway.

TO THE MAMMOTH-TORTOISE

OF THE MASCARENE ISLANDS.

BY AUSTIN DOBSON.

Tuque, Testudo, resonare septem
Callida nervis.   Hor. iii. 11.

Monster Chelonian, you suggest
　To some, no doubt, the calm,—
The torpid ease of islets drest
　In fan-like fern and palm ;

To some your cumbrous ways, perchance,
　Darwinian dreams recall ;
And some your Rip-van-Winkle glance,
　And ancient youth appal ;

So widely varied views dispose :
　But not so mine,—for me,
Your vasty vault but simply shows
　A Lyre immense,—*per se*,

A Lyre to which the Muse might chant
   A truly " Orphic tale,"
Could she but find that public want
   A Bard—of equal scale !

Oh, for a Bard of awful words,
   And lungs serenely strong,
To sweep from your sonorous chords
   Niagaras of song,

Till, dinned by that tremendous strain,
   The grovelling world aghast,
Should leave its paltry greed of gain
   And mend its ways. . . at last !

HOSPITAL·SKETCHES.

On ne saurait dire à quel point un homme, seul dans son lit et
malade, devient personnel. — BALZAC.

I.

FIRST IMPRESSIONS.

THE gaunt brown walls
Look infinite in their decent meanness.
There is nothing of home in the noisy kettle,
The fulsome fire.

The atmosphere
Is heavy and rank and unfamiliar.
Dressings and lint on the long, lean table—
Whom are they for?

The patients yawn,
Or lie as in training for shroud and coffin.
A nurse, in the corridor, scolds and wrangles.
It is grim and strange.

Far footfalls clank.

An old man waits with his leg unbandaged.

My neighbour chokes in the clutch of chloral . . .

What a curious world !

· II.

OPERATION.

You are carried in a basket,
  [Like a carcase from the shambles]
  To the theatre, a cockpit,
  Where they stretch you on a table.

Then they bid you close your eyelids,
  And they mask you with a napkin,
  And the anæsthetic reaches
  Thro' your senses, hot and subtle.

And you gasp, and reel, and shudder
  With a rushing, swaying rapture,
  While the voices at your elbow
  Thin, receding—fainter—farther.

K 2

Lights about you shower and tumble,
  And your blood seems crystallising,
  Edged and vibrant, yet within you
  Racked and hurried back and forward.

Then the lights grow fast and furious,
  And you hear a noise of waters,
  And you wrestle, blind and dizzy,
  In an agony of effort.

But a sudden lull accepts you,
  And you sound an utter darkness. . . . . .
  And awaken—with a struggle—
  On a hushed and curious audience.

III.

VIGIL

Lived on one's back
In the long hours of repose,
Life is a nightmare,
A grimy, a horrible nightmare.

Shoulders and loins
Ache, and the mattresses,
Horrid with boulders and hummocks,
Burn, and the gas,
An inevitable atom of light,
Haunts me, and stertorous sleepers
Snore me to madness.

All the old time
Surges before me malignant.
Old faces, old kisses, old songs,
Blossom derisive about me.
While the new days
Pass me in endless procession :
A pageant of shadows
Silently, staringly wending
On to the future.

Sleep comes at last—
Sleep, full of dreams and misgivings,
Broken with brutal and sordid
Voices and sounds that impose on me,
Ere I can wake to it,
The unnatural, intolerable day.

IV.

CLINICAL.

Hist? .   .   .   .

On through the corridor's echoes

Louder and nearer

Comes a great shuffle of feet.

Quick, every one of you,

Straighten your quilts, and be decent!

Here's the Professor.

In he comes first,

With the bright look we know

Under the broad, white brows, from the kind eyes

Soothing yet nerving you!   Here, at his elbow,

White-capped, white-aproned, the Nurse

Towel on arm, and her inkstand

Fretful with quills! .

Here, in the ruck, anyhow,

Surging along,

Louts, duffers, exquisites, students, and prigs—

Whiskers and foreheads, scarf-pins and spectacles!—

Hustle the Class !   And they ring themselves

Round the first bed, where the Chief

(His dressers and clerks at attention !)

Bends in inspection already.

So shows the ring

Seen, from behind, round a conjuror

Doing his pitch in the street !

High shoulders, low shoulders, broad ones and
     narrow ones,

Round, square, and angular, serry and shove ;

While from within a voice,

Gravely and weightily fluent,

Sounds ; and then ceases ; and suddenly

(Look at the stress of the shoulders !)

Out of a quiver of silence,

Over the hiss of the spray,

Comes a low cry, and the noise

Of breath quick intaken through teeth

Clenched in resolve.   And the Master

Breaks from the crowd, and goes,

Wiping his hands,

To the next bed, with his pupils

Flocking and whispering behind him.

Now one can see.

Case Number One

Sits rather pale, with his bedclothes

Stripped up, and showing his foot

(Alas for God's image !)

Swaddled in wet, white lint

Brilliantly hideous with red.

V.

ETCHING.

Two and thirty is the ploughman.

He's a man of gallant inches,

And his hair is close and curly,

    And his beard ;

But his face is wan and sunken,

And his eyes are large and brilliant,

And his shoulder-blades are sharp,

    And his knees.

He is weak of wit, religious,

Full of sentiment and yearning,

Gentle, faded—with a cough

    And a snore.

When his wife (who was a widow,
And is many years his elder)
Doesn't write, and that is always,
    He desponds.

If his melancholy leave him,
He will tell you pretty stories
Of the women that have wooed him
    Long ago ;
Or he'll sing of bonnie lasses
Keeping sheep among the heather,
With a crackling, hackling click
    In his voice.

VI.

CASUALTY.

As with varnish red and glistening
    Dripped the hair ; the foot was rigid ;
    Raised, he settled stiffly sideways :
You could see the hurts were spinal.

He had fallen from an engine,
    And been dragged along the metals.

It was hopeless, and they knew it :
So they covered him and left him.

As he lay, at fits half sentient,
   Inarticulately moaning,
   With his stockinged feet protruded
   Sharp and awkward from the blankets,

To his bed there came a woman,
   Stood and looked, and sighed a little,
   And departed without speaking,
   As himself a few hours after.

I was told it was his sweetheart.
   They were on the eve of marriage.
   She was quiet as a statue,
   But her lip was gray and writhen.

VII.

LYRIC.

Bleak's the night, and black and blustrous,
   But for sanitary reasons
   Someone dashes down the window,
   And the north wind enters blatant.

How the gaslight flares and flutters !
   Cards and tickets flicker madly,
   And the red quilts wave like banners ;
   And my fancies with the weather

Mingle swiftly—I am fronting,
   Glad and breathless and defiant,
   The immeasurable clamour
   Of the sea among the darkness.

Oh, the war of winds and waters !
   Low in heaven, afear'd and hurried,
   As the scudding wrack is rifted,
   Flits in fear a runaway moonlet.

Oh, the storm's exhilaration ! . . .
   I am back upon my pallet,
   And the tickets shake and flicker,
   And the quilts are blown like banners.

VIII.

INTERLUDE

Oh, the fun, the fun and frolic
　　That *the Wind that Shakes the Barley*
　　Scatters through a penny whistle
　　Tickled with artistic fingers !

Kate, the scrubber (eight and thirty,
　　Stout but sportive) foots it lightly,
　　Grinning like a ballet dancer,
　　Fixed as fate, upon her audience.

Stumps are shaking, crutch supported ;
　　Splinted fingers tap the rhythm ;
　　And a head all helmed with plasters
　　Wags a measured approbation.

Of their mattress-life oblivious,
　　All my mates, alert and cheerful,
　　Are encouraging the dancer,
　　And applauding the musician.

Dim the gas in the expression
    Of so many ardent smokers,
    Full of shadow lurch the corners,
    And the doctor peeps and passes.

There are, maybe, some suspicions
    Of an alcoholic presence . . .
    Now and then the dragon dozes.
    New Year comes but once a twelvemonth.

IX.

ROMANCE.

" Talk of pluck ! " pursued the sailor,
    Set at euchre on his elbow,
    " I was on the wharf at Charleston,
    Just ashore from off the runner.

" It was gray and dirty weather,
    And I heard a drum go rolling,
    Rub-a-dubbing in the distance,
    Awful dour-like and defiant.

" And between the bales of cotton,
    Mud, and chains, and stores, and anchors,
    Tramped a squad of battered scarecrows—
    Poor old Dixie's bottom dollar !

"Some had shoes, but all had rifles,
    Them that wasn't bald, was beardless.
    But the drum was rolling ' Dixie,'
    And they stepped to it like men, sir !

" Rags and tatters, belts and bayonets,
    On they tramped, the drum a-rolling,
    Mum and sour !—It looked like fighting,
    And they meant it too, by thunder ! "

X.

MUSIC.

Down the quiet eve,
Thro' my window, with the sunset,
Pipes to me a distant organ
Foolish ditties. . . .

I am well and young ;
Summer glares from road and footway,
And my heart is full of summer
Sap and sweetness.

In the quiet eve
I am waiting, I am dreaming . . .
Dreaming, and a distant organ
Pipes me ditties.

I can see the shop,
Cool with sprinkled blind and pavement,
Where she serves—her chestnut chignon
Fills my senses.

Oh, the sight and smell,
Quiet eve and sprinkled pavement !
In the distance pipes an organ . . . .
The sensation

Comes to me anew,
And my spirit for a moment,
Thro' the music, breathes the blessed
Air of London.

XI.

NOCTURN.

In the weary waste of midnight,
  When the shadow shuts and opens
  As the loud flames pulse and flutter,
  I can hear the cistern leaking.

Dripping, dropping, in a rhythm,
  Rough, unequal, half melodious,
  Like the measures aped from nature
  In the infancy of music ;

Tone and semitone emerging
  With significant inflections,
  Thro' surprising modulations,
  In barbaric turn and cadence ;

Still, irrational, persistent,
  Like the buzzing of an insect . . .
  I must listen, listen, listen,
  In a passion of attention,

Till it taps upon my heartstrings,
  And my very life goes dripping,
  Dropping, dripping, drip-drip-dropping,
  In the drip-drop of the cistern.

XII.

PASTORAL.

This is the spring.
Earth has conceived, and her bosom,
Quick with the summer, is glad.

Through the green land
Wind the gray roads, full of promise,
Peopled with wains, and melodious
With harness bells jangling,
Jangling and twangling rough rhythms,
To the slow march of the stately great horses
Whistled and shouted along !

White fleets of cloud,
Argosies heavy with fruitfulness,

L

Sail the blue peacefully.   Green flame the hedge-
  rows.
Blackbirds are bugling, and white in wet winds
Sway the slim poplars.
Placid in dreamy beatitude
Spread the sweet meadows, and viewless
Walks the mild spirit of May,
Visibly blessing the world.

Oh, the delight of the copses,
The unspeakable charm of the fields !
Loud lows the steer ; in the fallows
Rooks are alert ; and the brooks
Gurgle and tinkle and trill.   Thro' the gloamings,
Under the rare, shy stars,
Boy and girl wander
Dreaming in darkness and dew.

This is the spring.
A sprightliness feeble and squalid
Wakes in the ward, and I sicken,
Impotent, winter at heart.

XIII.

DISCHARGED.

Carry me out
Into the wind and the sunshine,
Into the beautiful world.

Oh, the wonder, the spell of the streets !
The stature and strength of the horses,
The echoing rustle of footfalls,
The flat roar and rattle of wheels !
A swift tram floats hugely upon us—
Is it a dream ?
The smell of the mud in my nostrils
Is brave—like a breath of the sea.

Just as of old,
Vaguely and strangely provocative,
Ambulant, undulant drapery
Flutters and beckons.   And yonder,
See, the white glint of a stocking !
Sudden, a spire,
Wedged in the mist !   Oh, the houses,

The long lines of lofty, gray houses,
Cross-hatched with shadow and light !
These are the streets.
Each is an avenue leading
Whither I will !

Free—!
Dizzy, hysterical, faint,
I sit, and the carriage rolls on with me
Into the wonderful world.

W. E. HENLEY,
The Old Infirmary, Edinburgh.

AUGUST, 1873—APRIL, 1875.

A LADY LAND LEAGUER.

BY F. MABEL ROBINSON.

DESPITE the wind and rain she had trudged over many miles of bog and hill, alone, and after nightfall; and though she had started with a heavy money bag she, at the time, had felt no fear; but now that her tramp was done and she was home again, a retrospective terror came over her and she burst into tears.

She was a single woman—a young lady she would have called herself—of thirty-five, and she lived quite alone on her own means. The means were small, but they sufficed her, for she had few and simple wants. For the two past years she had lived rent free in a tin house, provided by the Land League, and which stood solitary on a bleak Donegal hill side.

On the first of each month Miss Mulligan received a cheque for a hundred pounds, and then she set off on a car—she, herself, called it a "kyar"—and drove into town, cashed her cheque, and drove out again till the road became too rough for wheels; then she alighted, and money bag in hand she scrambled over the rough hillside in sun, or rain, or wind.

Every month she went the same round, over the mountain, over the cliff, down that deep dell, up the steep height of the opposite hill, stopping from time to time at a shelter of tin or wood or a hut of rough stones, and after each stoppage her bag was lighter by a fixed sum, duly acknowledged in her register. These money grants were always less than the recipients hoped to receive, and in return, Miss Mulligan got more complaints than thanks, coupled sometimes with a threat of "going in again." This menace she bore with equanimity, firstly, because since the evicted tenants had not the wherewithal to pay the arrears of rent due, they were mere empty words, and secondly, because the sole result to herself of their fulfilment would have been the saving of some fatigue and trouble. Indeed, sometimes her weariness so far surpassed her patriotic ardour, that she did wish the more isolated farmers could and would find some means of "going in."

Her round was a long one, and occupied two days, and on the second night her nerves always gave way, and she indulged herself in the luxury of a "rale good cry." The luxury was one she enjoyed keenly, and it was well within her means ; it cost her nothing, it injured no one, and as she had few diversions, she availed herself of it in unstinted measure, and frequently.

Without any well defined grievance, she suffered much from a sense of being hardly used. She was, in fact, unfitted by nature for her lonely life, and these desolate home-comings to the chill shelter, fireless and cold, overwhelmed her with a sense of misery. True she had dry clothing in her bedroom, abundance of wood and peat in her kitchen, and plenty of the raw materials for supper, but she was spent and weary, and the effort necessary to create her own comfort was too great for her : self-pity and tears were the most handy consolations, so she took them ; but the beneficial effect suggested by the adjective "good " were never among the outwardly discernible results of her weeping, she merely sobbed herself hysterical, went to bed cold and hungry, and passed a night of bodily discomfort and .often of mental terror.   Neuralgia and cold in the head generally made the following days of the month unendurable, and one or two of them were commonly spent in bed.

The distribution of funds was however not the sole nor the chief of Miss Mulligan's self-imposed duties ; true it was essential that this office should be performed by a person of unquestioned honesty, for by giving one sum and writing a receipt for a larger it would have been easy to appropriate a considerable portion of the fund, but honourable women are as plenteous as blackberries in September, and it was on her skill as a sewing teacher that Miss Mulligan valued herself—a perfect mastery of every variety of fine needlework was her one accomplishment.

Her father had been a grocer in a good way of business, and she had been educated in a convent, regardless of expense ; but whether the curriculum of that establishment was unscientific, or whether a certain haziness of brain unfitted her to grapple successfully with the deeper mysteries of the three R's, it is a fact that Miss Mulligan, though an intelligent

woman, was unable to distinguish between debit and
credit, or to make out her accounts in a manner that
conveyed any distinction between the items of receipt
and of expenditure to minds less subtle than her own.
Her conversation was no less involved than her book-
keeping ; her brain was active, and she had so many
ideas that, long ere she had traced one to its conclusion, something more brilliant or more opportune
diverted her, and this, in its turn, led to a fresh train
of thought, so that a chat with Miss Mulligan was a
fine intellectual exercise for those whose minds move
slowly and in familiar currents.   She never wrote a
letter less than twelve pages long, and as she enter-
tained a profound indifference for spelling and
punctuation, and a marked predilection for paren-
theses, her letters were not such that he who runs
may read.   They were, however, worth the trouble of
deciphering for her own sake, and often for the
subject matter.

Even in her wet clothing, muddy boots, and generally draggled and bespattered condition, Miss Mulligan was nice looking, and it was evident that she had
been extremely pretty in her day ; she had good

features, sweet, honest eyes, dark, abundant hair, and
a certain dignity of look and bearing—the hall mark
of single-mindedness and purity of purpose. No one
in the world could have thought ill of Miss Mulligan.

She, on the other hand, was prone to make harsh
judgments; like most hysterical persons she was
suspicious, seeing an enemy in everyone who was not
pronouncedly a friend ; she was resentful too, dearly
loving a grievance, and she had found one in the
supposition that her services were undervalued by her
male coadjutors. In this she was right, for perhaps
no human being estimates at its full value the
devotion of another's life, and the world is so used
to the self-abnegation of elderly young ladies that it
has come to believe that hardships and solitude are
sweet to spinsters over thirty, and that love of comfort and the force of habit are but slight bonds to a
woman when once the bloom and vigour of her youth
are past. Therefore, Miss Mulligan was justified
in thinking that the men undervalued her. They
did not realize that, after all, though she was five
and thirty, Miss Mulligan was still the centre of
creation to Miss Mulligan, nor did they comprehend

the extent of her self-abnegation in resigning the tempered joys of independent spinsterhood in Derry. Forgetting the monotony and isolation of the life she had taken up, they thought this industry a pleasant outlet for her pent up energies. They knew she was a good woman, but they found her hysterics trying, and her book-keeping intolerable, and though they were as convinced that the money was rightly spent as though this had been logically demonstrated, their faith was in no way proved by the elaborate sheets of figures she sent up in support of her statements. Faith did not satisfy Miss Mulligan, she demanded an act of understanding, and she alternated, according to her mood, in thinking the " men " extremely stupid, and trying to persuade herself that they wished to asperse her character.

On this wild night she had returned unusually cold and weary and depressed; she was worn out with battling against wind and gusty rain, and the many voices of the storm deprived her home of all peace and rest. Below in the valley the wind swept along with a rushing whirl, and ahead on the coast the waves beat and broke on the rocks with a deafening roar ; then a crash—then a sound like a sigh, or, as Miss Mulligan thought, a curse of impotent rage. Her shelter was quite a high-class affair ; it had a door with a knocker, a central passage ornamented with framed photographs of the Leaders, and terminating in a window of green glass and with two rooms on either side ; those to the right were devoted to her sewing school, and on the left were her bedroom and kitchen. The shelter had, in fact, been shown at an exhibition as the ideal Land League hut, and embellished by new paint and green ribbons had appeared quite a desirable residence. But the paint was now worn, ribbons no longer adorned the knocker, and the shelter, as is the nature of galvanized iron houses, was cold as a barn in winter, and a very oven in summer ; the stove was addicted to smoking, and the doors had "settled," so that two of them would not stay shut, while no effort of Miss Mulligan's sufficed to close the others, which were fixed immovably open. On such a night as this, the house too conveyed an unpleasant impression of fragility, and at every gust Miss Mulligan expected, or thought she expected, to be blown, house and all, into the valley. The windows strained and groaned beneath the assaults of the gale, and though Miss Mulligan had stopped the banging of the loose doors by propping them with chairs, they shook incessantly; the portraits of the Land Leaguers rattled briskly in their frames, and the knocker flapped solemnly at longer intervals.

Every inch of the house creaked and swayed, and over it all the rain clattered, noisy as pebbles on the iron roof, with a gusty rattle-splash-swish. At such seasons emotional persons, even in the happiest surroundings, feel the sob rise in their throats, and Miss Mulligan would have shed tears on such a night under any circumstances. Hungry, cold, weary, and forlorn, she wept from sheer misery and desolation, hugging the slur on her character theory till she really came to believe it. She had a vague feeling that all her discomfort, including the noisy and terrifying storm, was due to the "men," for it was under this abstract noun of multitude that she made mental reference to Callaghan. She held Callaghan especially responsible for her woes; firstly, because he was an old friend and ought to have known better—an unspecified charge which left Callaghan powerless to defend himself—

and, secondly, because he was that official of her
branch of the League with whom Miss Mulligan was
personally concerned. It was Callaghan who wrote
the cheques and did up the accounts, and who pro-
fessed himself unable to master her system of double
entry. In her present humour it did not take Miss
Mulligan long to fan up a bright flame of resentment
against Callaghan. She felt an imperative need of
quarrelling with some one, so she sat down at her
table and, sobbing the while, wrote a long letter to
Callaghan, charging him with accusing her of falsify-
ing the accounts. " When you *know* every penny has
been accounted for while as for myself I might
have had and did have a good home but for you not
that I regret what I have done for our poor people
but I am sorry that it has caused me to be accused
by them that can have no nobility in theirselves,
as they do not believe it in others but are
always willing to think the worst of others and
judge others by theirselves who would not for
the whole world take a penny of the poor
people that God knows! has a hard enough task
to support theirselves and could not do that if it was

not that I have taught the women to sew and knit and have given up every moment of my time to this for two years. Not that I wish to boast of this for I feels it to be no more than everyone should do but those that tries to do their Duty and looks for no Reward in this world should not be accused of doing things which the meanest robber would scorn to do his heart would blead to see the places that these poor people has gone into, and he would feel that a League should feel very sure of what the end of it will be before they ask poor people to give up the bad thing that they has and take the worse, but it is no use to write to one that living at his ease in town knows nothing of the dayly trowbles of the poor, that would bring tears to the eyes of a stone."

Having thus relieved her mind, Miss Mulligan wiped her eyes and went to bed; and, supported by an exultant conviction that she had vanquished Callaghan, escaped the influenza which formed the usual epilogue to her admistration of the fund. All through the week, her manner was marked by a certain indefinable elation, from which her pupils argued that she had found a husband. Nothing, in fact, was further from Miss Mulligan's mind than a wish to find a husband ; she had a poor opinion of the men, and was one of the many women who maintain that they can do aught that doth become a man, and a great many things besides.   In forming this judgment she had her own capacity for book-keeping in view, and contrasted the masterly ease with which she made out her accounts, with Callaghan's crass stupidity in comprehending them.   How Callaghan managed to keep the books of the League was past her comprehension, and as Miss Mulligan's accounts were by no means so unique, among the many sent in to him, as he could have wished, it was almost past his own comprehension also.

I am sorry to say that Miss Mulligan's letter did not impress him in at all the way that she had anticipated ; he was a big, jolly, good-natured man, who had never in his life been thrown much into the society of women, and the sex was to him a mystery, even more unfathomable than the chaos of Miss Mulligan's accounts.   He was content to accept both as simple substances defying analysis, but of by no means equal interest and value.   He was extremely soft-hearted towards women, young or old, pretty or ugly, all minor differences being merged in the pathetic mystery of their womanhood. Had Miss Mulligan come into his office he would at once have protested that he understood every item in her accounts, but her rigmarole did not carry the soften-ing effect of her presence, and Callaghan laughed. Yes, I am sorry to say he found Miss Mulligan's heart-wrung reproaches a very good joke. Still laughing, and in a teasing mood, he wrote to her— " My dear Miss Mulligan,—Surely 'tis you, not I, that are willing to believe the worst of others, but though I have no nobility I am not so stupid as to doubt yours. Believe me, I appreciate the sacrifices you have made, and never dreamt of accusing you of anything worse than an involved system of book-keeping. Never mind about debit and credit, I will try, by the items, to make a guess at which is which, but *do* try to keep the *Grant* money for the tenants distinct from the *Loan* for the sewing-girls, and which, you know, we may have to refund at any moment."

Now this was not quite honest of Callaghan. The

M

money, though nominally a loan, had been expended without thought of repayment, and there was no probability that the institution that had lent it would ever ask for its return ; but at the moment this note seemed to him the best way of explaining the need for keeping the accounts distinct, and also an excellent joke.

But " a jest's prosperity lies in the ear of him who hears it," and Callaghan's letter found Miss Mulligan in no joking humour. She read a slight between every word ; the whole tone of the letter seemed to her evidence of the basest ingratitude, and she was fairly frightened at the suggestion that the loan might be asked for at any time. The money was spent, and it was beyond her power to recall it. Packets of baby clothes and finely tucked nightdresses represented its value. These she removed from their shelves and laid one by one in a deal box till she had made up a package worth more than the forty-five pounds. Then she nailed up the box, addressed it to Callaghan, walked three miles to her carman, and bade him send round for it that very afternoon. When it was safely started, she sat down and made a second attempt to reduce the

iniquitous Callaghan. " If you had taken the trowble,"
she wrote, "to read what I have wrote you, you would
know that the money is all spent on calicoe and lace
and cannot be had back. It has all been spent on our
poor people but I don't wish that they or anyone else
who respects theirselves should put theirselves under
a compliment to any that grudges them their bread.
I am very sorry that I cannot send you the money
back but it is spent and the clothes I send you is
worth more. You will quite easy find market for them
in town as they are all very nice and you can get at the
shops 15 per cent higher than I have priced them but
I would rather sell at a loss than keep a loan that was
grudged. If I was a man I should behave different
and try to help women in their work instead of which
all you think of is how you can crush me. I don't
suppose the League is different to the rest. All men
are alike and would rather put us down than
help us."

Several tears blotted this epistle, and the trembling
handwriting testified to the emotion which had
inspired it. Until the answer came, Miss Mulligan felt
very down : the short winter days seemed shorter, the

long nights more interminable than before. Yet when
the time came for it to be possible for her to receive an
answer, Miss Mulligan prayed daily with beating heart
that the postman might not come, and when at last he
left a letter she hardly dared to open it. After long
speculation as to its possible contents she read : " My
dear Miss Mulligan,—This is too bad of you, and
makes me terribly ashamed of my little joke. I do
not want the money, and, if I did, how could I go
about hawking baby clothes ? After long study I still
can't discriminate between the ' shirts ' and ' shifts.'
Come up to town and find a market for them yourself,
and keep the proceeds for your industry, and please
come soon, as my furniture is covered with baby
clothes. You have really got to come, and must find
what consolation you may in the thought that you
have brought it on yourself."

A fortnight later the shelter was still empty and
Miss Mulligan still in town. ," The man," she admitted, had really been quite kind to her ; he had let
her hold a sale of work at his house, had been
induced to act unpaid commercial traveller in baby
linen, and had given a large order for knitted socks.

Despite her hatred of his sex, and her conviction of his desire to crush her, Miss Mulligan went everywhere under his escort, and endured his society with equanimity. But now the end of the month was come, and in two days the grant would be due. For some incomprehensible reason Miss Mulligan had found it impossible to broach the subject of her return, and she now walked quickly into Callaghan's office and said abruptly, " I'm going back to-morrow, so you may as well give me the money to take with me."

Callaghan rose and went over to the fire-place. " I shall feel very lonely without your scoldings," he said, looking at the blaze.

" Oh, I dare say ! Much heed you pay to 'em ! " said Miss Mulligan, bridling and laughing self-consciously.

" Did ever you ask me to do a thing that I didn't do it ? "

" Oh, that's your way," said Miss Mulligan airily, " you're a terrible man for the ladies."

Callaghan laughed, he was past forty, and growing stout, so he protested in only a half-hearted manner ;

and, as I said before, Miss Mulligan was very nice
looking. Her eyes now were just as soft and pretty
as though she had had the lightest possible hand in
flirtation, and the best conversational style. "There
is nothing too bad for you to believe of me," said
Callaghan, in a tone that challenged denial.

"Now I'm sure I never said that," said Miss Mulligan, with a provoking look that added, "though I
might have meant it."

"Well, you wrote it!" retorted Callaghan, "I've
got the letter!"

"Then just burn it at once," said Miss Mulligan,
inwardly very much pleased; "What would you
think if I kept all your cross letters—like an
informer!"

"You couldn't do that—I never wrote a cross word
to you; perhaps I will now I find out you destroy my
letters."

'Well, if they're nice I'll keep them for your biography." Miss Mulligan laughed a good deal at
this sally of hers; the notion of the biography was
clearly more fantastic in her eyes than in Callaghan's,
but he too laughed as he retorted—

" And I'll publish yours, that people may see what I've had to put up with ! "

" Then I'll write no more to be safe ! "

" Oh, that you will when you think my one aim is to crush you."

" Sure, I never said that ! "

Callaghan thrust his hand into his breast pocket—
" I'll show you the letter ! "

Miss Mulligan stayed him with her hand. " I didn't mean it. 'Tis dull there—one must have some diversion." The tears welled up into her pretty eyes.

" Is abusing your friend a diversion ? "

Miss Mulligan smiled : " Just to make him remember me."

" You might give him a stab for that reason."

She shook her head, laughing. " Hard words break no bones."

" They break hearts though," said Callaghan, re-turning to his desk. " However, you wouldn't mind if you broke mine, would you ? "

" Indeed, but I would ! "

" Well, there's but one way out of it now," said

Callaghan, a dusky, middle-aged blush suffusing his features. " You must do that or be my wife."

Miss Mulligan drew in her breath with a sob. " I must stay with the tenants till they get back."

Callaghan bowed his head ; he respected that sentiment. " And after ? "

" Well—after," said Miss Mulligan.

A COMFORTER.

BY THE BISHOP OF BEDFORD.

I WAS so weary with the strife and din,
　　And strange sad questionings that, night and day
　　Clamouring for answer, would not pass away,
And all the mystery of grief and sin
That smote upon my heart and entered in,
　　I could have craved to flee from out the fray,
　　And, in some rural home withdrawn, allay
This restless heat, and sweet contentment win.
Then came to me a little stranger child,
　　With wide blue eyes and wealth of sunny hair,
　　And climbed upon my knee, and nestled there :
And as in loving trustfulness she smiled,
　　And laid her golden head upon my breast,
　　I had my fill of comfort and of rest.

A WOMAN'S SONG!

BY CLEMENT SCOTT.

I.

SHE took her Song to Beauty's side,
Where riches are, and pomp, and pride,
Among the world, amidst the crowd,
She found out hearts by sorrow bow'd ;
There midst a dream of lights and dress,
She saw the pain of loveliness !
Her voice's magic held a tear,
She made the weary ones draw near,
And all the Passions of the throng
Were melted into Peace by Song !

II.

She took her Song along the Street,
And hushed the beat of passing feet ;
So tired toilers stopped to fill
Their hearts with music at her will !

She sang of Rest to weary feet,
Of sea-moan, and of meadow-sweet !
Her voice's pleading stilled the stir,
And little children wept with her !
So all their hate, and grief, and pain,
She softened into Love again !

III.

She took her Song to those who rest
Safe in the clasp of Nature's breast !
Amidst the graves, along the shore
Washed with salt tears of nevermore !
And then she sang, " How long ! how long !
" Before we hear that perfect song,
"That angel-hymn, that mystic strain,
"When those who loved shall love again ;
" When Life's long trouble shall be blest
"With Music of Eternal Rest !"

April 30*th*, 1887.

THREE UNPUBLISHED LETTERS OF GENERAL GORDON

To his old Friend, the late COLONEL C. ELWYN HARVEY, R.E.

Contributed by A. EGMONT HAKE.

~~~~~~~~~~

<div align="right">

7, CECIL STREET, STRAND,

16.1.77.

</div>

MY DEAR CHARLES,

I am not going back to the Khedive, and my future is rather hazy. I am in town, for a short time, but cannot say for certain, for how long, however I am sure to hear you are in town, and we will be sure to meet. About the dining out, I cannot stand it anywhere, puts me into a fidget, having a dinner hanging over one's head, so you will not press that question. I hope Mrs. Harvey and your boy is well, and with kind regards, Believe me in haste.

<div align="center">

Yours sincerely,

C. E. GORDON.

</div>

<div align="center">

[*Reproduced in facsimile.*]

</div>

7. Cecil Street
Strand.
16 . 1 . 77

My dear Charles.

I am not going back
to the Khedive, and my
future is rather hazy. I
am in town, for a short
time, but cannot say for
certain, for how long, how-
-ever I am sure to hear
you are in town, & we will
be sure to meet about
the dining out, I cannot
stand it, any where, just
me

into a fidget, having a dinner
hanging over one's head, so
you will not press that
question. I hope Mrs Harvey
& your boy is well & with
kind regards Believe me
in haste Yours sincerely
C.E. Gordon.

My dear Charles.

I am sorry not to have seen you, ere I leave, which I do for Cairo, on the 31st inst—. I am so much occupied that I have no time to write at length, & tried to cry off. but H. H. would not have it, so I am going. Kind regards to Mrs Charles & your boy

Yours sincerely my dear Charles

C. H. Gordon.

7, CECIL STREET, STRAND,
25.12.76.

MY DEAR CHARLES,

I arrived in London last night, and am not at all certain of my future, for I have promised to come back to Cairo in three weeks, and then I have repented. I was pressed into it by Khedive, who is *bien malheureux*, and I did not like to desert a sinking ship.

How is Mrs. C. Elwyn? I hope well. How is that place Tring? I used to be sick of the very name. With very kind regards,

Believe me, my dear Charles,

Yours sincerely,

C. E. GORDON.

7, CECIL STREET, STRAND,
24.1.77.

MY DEAR CHARLES,

Sorry not to have seen you, ere I leave, which I do for Cairo, on the 31st inst. I am so much occupied that I have not time to write at length. I tried to cry off, but H. H. would not have it, so I am going. Kind regards to Mrs. Charles and your boy.

Yours sincerely, my dear Charles,

C. E. GORDON.⁻

[Reproduced in facsimile.]

ON THE SHELF.

BY ARTHUR GAYE.

I AM one of the rare and thrice fortunate beings who, so far from being ashamed of their great age, actually glory in it themselves, and are commended for it by others. This amiable characteristic I share with wine, fiddles, and, to the best of my belief, with none beside. Nay, I enjoy a distinct advantage over even these. There is a limit to the desirable antiquity of all that is vinous. The prime is reached and should never be passed, or it will too surely degenerate into something which savours less and less of vinosity. Good wine, it is true, needs no bush, and good old wine wants a champion even less; but not all the vegetation in Christendom can successfully proclaim a liquor which has begun to lose its virtue, be it never so patriarchal. It is fit only for base uses, and ultimately becomes vinegar or worse. So, too, with the masterpieces of the Cremona workshops. The

handiwork of Stradivarius and the Amati is, to begin
with, a good deal younger than myself, though, I
freely admit, of a very respectable age. Then again,
its authenticity is constantly being called in question.
Perhaps not a score of persons within the length and
breadth of this country can arbitrate with authority
where a reputed " Strad " is on its trial. Of the fifty-
eight or seventy pieces of wood which, as I am told,
go to form it, only an expert can decide whether all,
and if not all, how many or how few are what they
pretend to be. The purfling, for example, may be
genuine, and the finger-board and the sound-post, but
what of the scroll and the varnish ? In any case the
bridge must have had many predecessors, and strings,
even the Roman, which, they tell me, are most highly
prized, must be renewed at frequent intervals. But
granted that the whole and all its parts are un-
doubted original, and un-improved product of the great
Antonius himself, yet, after all, the really appreciative
admirers of the instrument must be confined to the
initiated few. It can be so easily imitated to delude
the vulgar ; nay more, its counterfeits are the back-
bone of a regularly organized trade. With me and

my congeners it is not so. Wine may turn sour and
fiddles may be forged; but each new year only adds
to my value and mellowness, and the sincerest form
of flattery cannot so much as approach me, for I am
imitator proof. Need I say more to disclose my
identity? I am an old book.

Where was I born? Well, I do not pretend to be
a Caxton, or even from the press of Aldus Manutius,
or of Elzevir. A man may be venerable without having reached the age of Methuselah, and a book may
well inspire a notable degree of interest, and yet have
not issued in the first instance from the famous house
in Westminster. To tell the truth, I first saw the
light, or what little there was of it to see, in a damp
cellar, for printing, in my day, was still looked at somewhat askance, and, albeit its profits were handsome, the
practice of it was not all plain sailing, or even devoid
of actual danger. As for my precise date, you will
find it, if you are inquisitive, in its proper place on my
title-page. I have said already that I am proud of it,
quite as proud, after my kind, as you are of your
power to destroy space by conversing with your
friend in Oceania, or to blow up your friends and foes

with the latest development of dynamite. I belong,
you see, to a constructive age, while yours, I take it,
is in the main of a destructive tendency; yet I am
presumptuous enough to fancy that I shall survive
when you and your explosives have long passed into
oblivion.

I was a long time about coming into the world; I
made my entry letter by letter and line by line.
Perhaps that is why my pages have lasted so long.
For many previous years, of course, I had already
existed in manuscript, such manuscript as no mortal
pen could in these days design. Copies of me were
made by patient hands, but Gothenburg's invention
soon put an end to the art of the copyist, and, moreover, it is with my life in print that I am now concerned
to entertain you. How well I remember that small
underground chamber in which I gradually assumed
my present character! You are wont to speak in these
times of "rushing" into print; there was little enough
of rush about it in my day, the process being only somewhat more expeditious than the original writing by
hand. Once perfected in the fount, however, I could
be multiplied at pleasure, not indeed at the terrific

N

rate of modern literature, but yet very much more
speedily than had been anyhow possible hitherto.
Half a page of me, perhaps, would be printed in the
time which you now occupy in striking off a volume,
though I do not know that you are altogether gainers
by this marvellous acceleration of speed.   Then, too,
it must be borne in mind that I am not in crown
octavo, but in folio.   Most of us were folios in the
early years of the press, when Plancus was consul.
But of that more anon.

   Whose was the inner consciousness from which I
was in the first instance evolved I do not greatly care
to set down.   Scarcely one of you, probably, would
recognize the name ; you may find it in catalogues of
scarce books, but in this degenerate age it is not, I
freely admit, one to conjure with.   In my very
youngest days, that is to say, when first I knew myself
to be a complete MS., long, long before my era of
leaded type, I took a pardonable pride in the subject
which I was originally designed to elucidate and adorn.
That pride is to this day not wholly obsolete in me,
but it is decidedly obsolescent.   In common with
many other literary efforts of my own standing, I am a

Romance of Chivalry, consisting in a voluminous
compilation of the jests of once famous Knights, and
concluding with sundry maxims intended to awaken
the chivalrous spirit anew. I am not indeed the rare
edition of Amadis de Gaul, but I may fairly claim to
be one of that ilk. The aim of my author has not
been realized. While there is a good deal within my
covers that would do honour to any age and any land,
there is also not a little that, in my opinion, although
I herein speak against myself, has very wisely been
abandoned and forgotten. Many of the principles,
for example, in vogue among those Knights of the
Round Table, whose exploits are familiar to you in the
melodious Idylls of one of your best poets, will be up-
held by right-thinking men until the end of time. But
their principles, as we well know, did not always
coincide with their practice, and these heroes, and
others who followed them, lapsed not seldom into the
grosser errors of frail humanity. Hence it is that I
contain divers passages which might with advantage
be expunged, though I cherish no vain hope that any
editor will ever think it worth his while to bring out
an expurgated version of me. To redress the wrongs

of the weak and oppressed, to hold fast by the Truth, to endure hardness for the Right, to take heart of Grace and stand up valiantly against the evil-doer—— verily these be one and all excellent features in a man. But it grieves me that not a few of my venerable pages exhibit a strong confusion of chivalry and licence. I am liberal enough to recognize the fact that the doughty knights, whose feats are recounted in me, were on the whole considerably inferior to other and more modern champions, whose names, it is true, are unknown to fame, but whose deeds nevertheless evince a nobler spirit, and belong, as it seems to me, to a far higher order of chivalry than anything that I myself was penned and printed to illustrate. Having lived through many phases of social life and carefully noted them all, I think, for instance, that the knights who minister to the grievous necessities of sick children in the East End of London are, to speak truth, a good many rungs on the ladder of true nobility above the mailed warriors who spent their days in tilting for the favour of fair maidens. I sometimes feel that the fate which overtook the library of the Knight of the Sorrowful Countenance was on the whole not much worse than it deserved. This, of course, is in my melancholy and self-abasing moments. At other times it gratifies me to remember that I can offer some really sound, worthy, and remunerative reading. And even in my most disconsolate moods I am apt to dwell with satisfaction on the shrewd Spaniard's comforting conclusion, borrowed, however, from a more ancient source : No hay libro tan malo que no tenga alguma cosa buena.—Even the worst book has *some* good in it. A fallacious remark, probably, like most sayings proverbial or epigrammatic, but it consoles me notwithstanding, call it vanity or what you will.

It is possible that you may be interested to know something as to my appearance without and within. There is a certain sameness about the covers of volumes of my date, but it is a sameness which does not necessarily become a weariness. There is nothing fantastic about them, nothing crude, nothing loud or extravagant. The marvellous freaks of the binder's art, which I have observed during the present century, have absolutely nothing in common with the sober livery which obtained for the most part in my own

day. Such miserable subterfuges also, if you will
excuse the term, as cloth, boards, and leatherette,
were yet a long way off. If my comrades and myself
cannot boast the magnificent exteriors which were
designed and executed by some of the later French
and Italian craftsmen, we have at least much that is
substantial, and, witness our longevity, durable to
show. Our backs and sides were, at any rate, made
of leather (and, as all men know, there is nothing like
leather) and solid to boot. Our very size lent us
externally some importance. A well-bound folio
means a good deal of binding material, and neither
quantity nor quality in our case was stinted. We
represent, each one of us, several square feet of
outside, and every inch was clad in the bravest. The
men who produced us (I mean our form, not our
matter) took the greatest pride in their work. That
work was not in so many different hands as the
editing of books now is. Printer, binder, publisher,
and seller, were all one and the same worthy soul,
under whose watchful eye each department wrought
its special share of labour. The profits of the trade
were encouraging, and its various details were

honestly, thoroughly, sometimes even lavishly, carried out; nothing was scamped. Whether the actual writers were satisfied with their publishers or not, in my century, I am not prepared to say. Probably, like their successors, they were not; perhaps they too, even as one of your own modern authors, were of opinion that Barabbas was a publisher. Be that how it may, they could certainly never find fault with the outward appearance of their histories or romances when they finally issued from the press. Externally they were, they are, all that the soul of author could desire. But, as I said before, I and my contemporaries had, most of us, existed for many generations in MS., or ever we were advanced to the dignity of type.

I confess to a feeling of comfortable security, not unmixed with a sense of superiority to those around me, when I take note of the kindly pressure of my sturdy leathern sides. Time-worn no doubt they are, time-worn and travel-stained, and here and there are indications of visits on the part of an attentive but voracious and coleopterous little friend, whose name is well known in libraries. I do not grudge him,

however, an occasional meal at my expense, and I
wish him happy digestion. It would have been strange
indeed had I come down through this long range of
years without betraying some slight symptoms of wear
and tear. But I am solid enough still as to my outer
skin, and I feel that I shall be solid to the last. Yes,
here and there on my ample covers you may detect
the friendly worm-hole; my edges may be a trifle
bowed with age, and the ribs on my broad back may
have lost a little of their whilom glory. But what of
that. The years that I have been cased in leather
are to be reckoned by centuries. And the colour of
me—can you anywhere match this fine deep russet,
which nothing save length of years and soundness of
constitution combined can hope to produce? It was
once whispered, in my hearing, that a spray of scarlet
geranium carelessly laid upon me would create a
study worthy the brush of the greatest of painters. A
beautiful old tome I have many a time been called,
for the warm, mellow colouring of my back and sides
alone. Add my strength and symmetry to my beauty,
and you have something, I humbly submit, which
cannot easily be equalled, let alone excelled, in the
matter of book-binding.

When you shall have sufficiently admired my outer charms, let me invite you to open me and feast your eyes upon the grace and grandeur that are contained within. Here too, of course, some little allowance must be made for the ravages of time. I do not pretend that my every page is spotless or free from the inevitable ills to which a book of my age is unhappily heir. Now and again you will certainly come upon the traces of the tiny borer and the pestilential dog's-ear. A few pages of my fine Dutch paper are unacountably yellow, and one or two have been patched, cleverly enough, but not so cleverly as to deceive myself. But, these insignificant blemishes apart, where, I should like to know, will you find among your own printed volumes such type, so clear and so regular as mine? I have no patience with your wretched little duodecimos and diamond editions, which serve only to injure young eyes, and baffle those that are old. What wonder that the readers of these days are constrained to avail themselves often in youth and almost without exception in middle age of artificial lenses, in order to spell through a page at all. Books in my time were not so plenty by many degrees as now, but they could at least be read with tolerable comfort. Fine black letters and capitals in royal scarlet; these are what meet your eye as you turn my leaves. The initial letters of my chapters, you will observe, are genuine works of art. I do not owe them to the skill of my printer, for the spaces were left blank, and were afterwards filled in with designs to suit the taste and fancy of my first purchaser. He employed a deft illuminator to give me these finishing touches, and I think you must admit that his confidence was not misplaced. Each several initial is a perfect picture in itself, and, as I have overheard it said, affords a pleasant relief to the reader's eye from the monotony of the printed character. You cannot fail, again, to notice and, I should hope, to admire also, the elegant little tail-pieces, which are continually cropping up. In truth, look where you will, at the beginning of chapter or at end, you must needs recognize in me a grand and edifying specimen of the art introduced into this land by the laborious Caxton and continued by Wynkyn de Worde and his successors unto this day.

Whilst passing through the press I was accustomed

to take note of sundry manners and customs affected
by the printing folk, most of which have long since
gone out of use, and are known now, if known at all,
only by vague tradition.   In the first place, every
printing-house went by the name of a " chappel."   I
have heard it said, but with what truth I know not,
that Caxton set up a press within the precincts of
Westminster Abbey, nay in one of the chapels themselves, and hence the term.   Each workman, or
compositor, as you call him in these days, was styled
a " member of the chappel," and the oldest freeman
was the " father."   Very strict discipline was maintained in these societies, and various penalties were
imposed when a " chappel " law or custom was
infringed.   Some of the commoner breaches sound
quaint enough to modern ears, as also does the
penalty, oddly termed a " solace."   I can call to mind
several instances.   Thus swearing, fighting, abusive
speech, or giving the lie in the " chappel " involved a
" solace."   So, too, for a stranger to come to a
compositor and enquire if he had news of such and
such a galley at sea.   If any man brought a wisp of
hay directed to a pressman (we may guess the gentle

insinuation) he was straightway " solaced." And if
the fines were not religiously paid the delinquent was
placed with scant ceremony on the " correcting
stone," and the amount due was collected in stripes.
Each new workman had to pay his " benvenue " or
entrance-fee, and, until he had paid it, took no benefit
of " chappel " money or other benefits accruing to the
recognized members of the craft. And, finally, there
was the so-called " wayzgoose," or printers' feast,
which still survives, and is useful, if for no other purpose, at least as exercising the wits of the etymologists.
Indeed, if by chance you have a turn for roots and
derivations, you will find in the various printers' terms
a wide field for testing your powers of extraction and
assimilation. You might, for example, discover for us
the true source of the (printers') devil, for I suppose you
will not rest satisfied any more than myself with the
tradition which makes the first of the tribe a lineal
descendant of one De Ville, who came over in the
Conqueror's train in company with the first D'Ash-
wood and the original D'Umpling. Possibly there is
more of truth in what an old writer says of this
opprobrious ekename : " These boys do in a printing-

house commonly black and dawb themselves, whence
the workmen do jocosely call them devils, and sometimes spirits, and sometimes flies." But I leave the
nut to your cracking.

In the course of a long life I have naturally
experienced many vicissitudes of fortune. I have
been in many countries and more hands. I can
remember on one occasion a long visit to Spain, a
country interesting to me as the birthplace of many
Romances of Chivalry, and no less interesting, I
trust, to you as having been the first land (though by
some the palm is given to Italy) to establish a
Hospital. It was not, we may be sure, so complete
or so well organized an institution as many a one, in
these more enlightened days, to be found in the
great English capital. Still it was a beginning, and
honour to whom honour is due, whether Spaniard or
Italian. It has been my lot to witness more than
once or twice the horrors of war and pestilence, and
it grieves me to reflect how many a noble life has
been lost through lack of appliances and skill which
you more fortunate moderns have at your very doors.
I can well remember the time when charms and

incantations supplied, in great measure, the place of
drugs, when the poor wrestled with the Rider on the
Pale Horse, in wretched hovels, untended and
uncared for, and sick children had none to minister
to their necessities. Truly, if to weep were one of a
book's prerogatives, I could shed copious tears over
the pathetic ignorance and superstition of the past,
whenever I contrast them with the comfort, the
unwearied ministrations, and the skilful treatment,
which are within the reach of the afflicted poor,
whether infant or adult, of to-day.

I have had in my time many masters, and yet
have remained for as much as a century in one
family, handed down religiously from father to son.
To say that I have been widely or deeply read
would, perhaps, not be within the limits of strict
veracity. A good many of my possessors were
unable to read at all, and those of them who were
competent to decipher me have, for the most part,
with sad want of taste, contented themselves with
regarding me in the light of an interesting fossil,
worth having but only to be looked at. My market
value, however, has always been a constant quantity ;

nay more, as I grow in years, so also do I rise in price. Dainty fingers have turned my pages, assisted not seldom by others of less delicate mould, and I have sometimes heard whispered over me words which sounded like *O gran bontà de' cavalieri antichi*, but I fancy they were meant merely as a cloke of ignorance, or to air a slender acquaintance with a foreign language. At all events I feel quite certain that in my MS. days, when it required the labour of years to reproduce me, my contents were conned and digested much more assiduously than they have ever been since I was promoted to the honour of print.

Though in one sense undoubtedly our natural home and rest-house it is humiliating even to a book to lie perpetually on the shelf. For years together I have reposed in that haven, and have acquired sometimes a coating of dust which weighs upon me. Not indeed that I bear any ill-will towards the quiet dust, on the contrary, I enjoy it in moderation, and I yield to no book, ancient, mediæval, or modern, in my abhorrence of the housemaid; that irrepressible, unreasoning, irreverent, bugbear of the library. From time to time I have emerged from this obscurity, and I must

admit that I have invariably been treated with the
greatest respect—the respect due to age, but not
always accorded even by those who know that I
belong to a period in which the printing-press was
still a novelty, and its children costly to come by. In
my later years I have been much sought after by
collectors, and thus have many times changed hands,
always, however, maintaining a good reputation for rarity
and representing therefore a high commercial value.
But it was a gruesome hour for me when I first
became acquainted with the hammer of the auctioneer.
To lie cheek by jowl with a heap of flimsy novels, or
to be jostled by ill-printed, meanly bound, editions of
popular authors, was a strange and melancholy
experience for one, like myself, accustomed to the best
and most ancient folio society. It was some consolation on these occasions to find myself now and then
within hail of an Elzevir in similarly reduced circumstances, and to join my lamentations with his anent
the decadence of the book-world. Adversity, as your
proverb runs, makes strange bedfellows ; and the
truth of the adage has ere now come safely home to
me when I have discovered in my next neighbour an

octavo copy of the pleasantries of one Joseph Miller, or the Adventures of an obscure person entitled Tom Jones. No true aristocrat of bookdom, I fancy, but would shudder in such company.

Latterly, however, I have ceased to grieve over the inevitable ; perhaps it is resignation, perhaps the weariness and apathy of age. It even amuses me in a mild way to hear myself described in the catalogues as "this very scarce and curious work, a good tall copy in old stamped calf binding (a few MS. notes on the margin in a very old hand, part of one leaf deficient) splendidly printed in red and black ink on thick vellum paper, and embellished with a woodcut title and very numerous large ornamental capitals.' I know that I shall be knocked down to a dealer or a collector, neither of whom has the slightest intention of mastering my contents. Once valuable for the information and sentiments I contain, I am now prized merely for my antiquity and excellent state of preservation. Even these characteristics are only regarded as entitling me to "fetch," such is the slang phrase, so many coins of the realm, and breathing this mercenery atmosphere I suppose I have caught

o

something of the spirit of the auction-room myself.
At any rate I do listen with some little interest to the
course of the bidding, and the fall of the hammer
strikes somewhat less of contempt and disgust into
my ancient heart when the competition for me has
been more than usually brisk, and I have changed
hands at what is vulgarly called a high figure.   My
public appearances, however, have of late years been
so many that the excitement of the auction must
needs soon pall upon me.

   At the present moment, and for some months
past, lying idle and unnoticed in the back room of a
celebrated dealer, in readiness for a customer who
declines to appear, I have employed my leisure in
jotting down these few notes of my life.   This is how
it all came about.   I have for society just now several
highly respectable old volumes, and during the night,
when we are free from intrusion and the abominably
rough handling which falls to our share during the
day, we are fond of talking over old times together.
It makes our present condition a trifle less monoton-
ous, to compare notes.   A few nights ago it was
suggested by a very worthy Amsterdam quarto, that

one of us should set down a few of his experiences for the benefit of the outside world. He went on to propose that the perpetrator of these autobiographical lucubrations should be myself, and he quoted as one reason for his preference a saying which he declares to be current in his own country. I should tell you that both he and the rest of my comrades are well aware that I set some store by my handsome binding. So, in his somewhat uncouth, but always kindly Netherlandish fashion, he maintained that I was the proper person to undertake the task, because "een zindelijk kleed is eene goede aanbeveling," or rendered into intelligible language, "a smart coat is a good letter of introduction." Though the compliment was not precisely in the vein of my own chivalrous up-bringing, I somehow, could not find it in my heart to say him nay, and the proposal being seconded by a shrivelled Aldine and endorsed by the rest of the company, all, by the way, more or less, in tatters, I agreed to do my best in the direction indicated.

The Hollander, who happens to be a scarce edition of the life of the famous Boerhaave, then mentioned

O 2

that he contained between his two rather squat covers
a vast store of antiquated information on the subject
of Medicine. This led him to express a wish that
I should introduce into my reminiscences a word or
two touching the wonderful expansion in these days
of medical knowledge and benevolence. He spoke
especially of the Hospitals for Children, and regretted
that the great Dutch physician could not see a sight
which would have gladdened his eyes, but which was
not destined to be visible till many a long year after
his death. The Quarto, whose heart is as sound as
his binding is the reverse, begged me to draw attention to the great need which exists of further develop-
ing the system. He cited several of his guttural
native proverbs to prove that the loving care of
children, and especially of children who are sick
or poor, is the duty of all Christian men and
women. It appears that he lived for some time
in Shadwell, and there became aware of the
Hospital which for several years has been
devoted to the reception of the suffering little ones
who dwell in the East. Tell the world, he said, what
an incalculable blessing such a refuge becomes in

such a wilderness, provided as it is with everything that science can suggest for the alleviation of the pains of these little patients, and wanting only the co-operation of the well-to-do classes to extend its blessings yet more widely. "*Grijp moed,*" he concluded, "and write your best."

These remarks being received with great applause, expressed in the book-world, by subdued clapping of leathern sides, I gave my promise that they should be introduced as nearly verbatim as my knowledge of the Dutch language permitted. And, in truth, you have here the gist of my stout friend's highly praise-worthy sentiments. Allow me to commend them to your very particular and appreciative notice.

I have run on, pray do not say "maundered" or "drivelled," somewhat beyond, I fear, the limits of your patience. Kindly forgive the garrulity of age, and let also the worthiness of my object plead some excuse. Probably you are of opinion that you your-self could do a great deal better than this, did you essay to speak "like a book." Try by all means, and my best wishes go with you. But whatever you write, fail not, I beseech you, to edge in a word for the Sick

Children, and the noble Hospital, whose staff of doctors and Nurses, daily and nightly, play the good Samaritan to them. Think of your own little ones, whose lightest malady is so carefully tended and cured : and then think of, and help those other little ones, dragged up in " poverty, hunger, and dirt," the misery of whose sick beds can only be relieved if you consent to stretch out the helping hand.